THE LAST RIDE

The Saga of Mister Bill

by William Stafford Sessoms

The contents of this work, including, but not limited to, the accuracy of events, people, and places depicted; opinions expressed; permission to use previously published materials included; and any advice given or actions advocated are solely the responsibility of the author, who assumes all liability for said work and indemnifies the publisher against any claims stemming from publication of the work.

All Rights Reserved
Copyright © 2024 by William Stafford Sessoms

No part of this book may be reproduced or transmitted, downloaded, distributed, reverse engineered, or stored in or introduced into any information storage and retrieval system, in any form or by any means, including photocopying and recording, whether electronic or mechanical, now known or hereinafter invented without permission in writing from the publisher.

Dorrance Publishing Co
585 Alpha Drive
Pittsburgh, PA 15238
Visit our website at www.dorrancebookstore.com

ISBN: 978-1-6853-7380-1
eISBN: 978-1-6853-7694-9

This is the story of Cowboy Bill, born on a dusty farm where his father and mother grew corn and beans. They had two cows and a bull. They just showed up one night and stayed. They had no brand on their hips, so Father said we will give them a home. He made a branding iron and formed it to read "A.S.B.," which stood for Allen, Smith, Bill.

Mother said they came from above. At that time, I wasn't sure what she meant. Since Mother said it, I was sure she was right. We plowed the fields in the summer time with a mule that Father had bought with money that he made cleaning out the stables in the town's horse barns. He worked until he was given the mule.

We planted beans in between the corn stalks. There had to be enough to get us through the winter. We had a lot of corn and beans to ward off hunger during the snowy days and night. Mama made us shirts and pants and a dress for herself from some fabric that she had kept for many years. Jackets were made from the skin of whatever Dad killed on his hunting trips.

He downed a few trees that we could chop up and pile near the door for cooking and warmth during the cold winter nights. I would load it on a drag that Millie would pull to the house.

Dad would say, "Son, I don't know what I would do if you were not here to help me." I think he said that just to get me to work harder.

The years went by. They didn't change much. We were happy in our house on the farm. Dad did not want Mama to work in the fields. He said outside work is for us men. Mama and Dad would hug a lot, and sometimes Mama would kiss him on the cheek.

Dad would smile and say, "I love you, my dear." Then he would look at me and say, "One day a girl will kiss you on the cheek and you will say, 'I love you, my dear.'"

When I was about twelve-years-old, Dad came back from town, which was about fifteen miles away. He would make it there and back in daylight hours. I guess he did not want us to be alone after dark. Each trip he made, he would take some corn and beans. Mama said he would buy a horse with the money he made from the sale of corn and beans. Then one day he came home with a Palomino. He named her Pal.

He said, "Son, your job will be to feed her and take care of her."

Oh, how I loved that job! I did not think of it as work. It was a pleasure each day to water and feed this beautiful horse. Sometimes at night, before I would fall asleep, I would think and say to myself how lucky I am to be here with Mama and Dad, and of course Millie and Pal.

Mama would read from a book each night. The book she called the Bible. Stories of love and courage and a man called Jesus. Her voice was soft and kind as she read to Dad and me.

Then one night she said, "Son, I want you to read some each night." Mama, I can't read. She said, " I will teach you how." So each night Mama would read from the book, and I would read from the book. After a few nights, I could read a few words. I was hooked on learning words.

One day Dad came back from town and handed me three books. On the cover of each book were a horse and a cowboy with a pistol on each hip. They were marked with a one, two, three.

Dad said, "Read number one first. Read it over and over until you read it well. Mother will help you to learn the words." The titles of the books were *The Adventures of Cowboy Bill.*

Most every night Mama would teach me words from the book. She liked the words, "the Lord is my shepherd; Love one another." She said to me always be faithful to Jesus, our Lord.

One day when we were planting beans, Dad said, "Son, go into the house and bring me my rifle." I ran into the house, grabbed the rifle, and gave it to Dad. As the rider and horse came closer, we could see blood on his vest. The

The Last Ride

horse stopped in front of the watering trough to take a drink. Dad rushed over to help the cowboy out of the saddle.

"Son, take care of his horse. I will take this man inside and see to his wounds." I led the horse to a feeding trough and gave her some corn. She needed currying down and cleaned up. I took her saddle off, got a bucket of water and a brush, rubbed her down, and curried her coat. Then I put her in the fence with Pal and Millie. They seemed to like each other.

Mama came out the door. She yelled, "Son, get a bucket and go to the spring house and then bring it inside. Papa needs to clean this man's wounds." When I got to the house with a bucket of water, I could see that the stranger was sleeping, I thought. Mama said, "Get me my bottle on the shelf over there." Dad tore up a shirt that I had outgrown and cleaned the wound. Then he poured some whisky on it and turned him over and did the same again.

I heard him tell Mama, "The bullet went clean through him, which might be a blessing." He bandaged him up, and Dad said, "Let's pray for him."

Mama took his hand, my hand, Dad's hand. "Jesus," she said, "here lays one of your children. Raise him up with your healing grace. I pray this in the name of Jesus." Each day she would call us in, hold his hand and our hands, and say the same prayer. Jesus here he's one of your children. Raise him up with your healing grace.

Then one morning before dawn, we heard a voice say, "Hello, hello." Dad jumped out of bed and slowly peeped out the door. The man was awake. He looked at Dad and then at his body. He stared at Dad and said, "Did you do this for me?"

"Yes," Dad replied. By that time, Mama was in the room and I was in the doorway. Dad held Mama close and said to me, "Come over here, son." He looked at the stranger and said, "We did it for you." Tears wet his eyes, and drops ran down his face.

Mama brought him some bean soup and said, "Eat and rest." After he had eaten and drank some water, Dad got his bottle down.

"First take a drink of this," which he gladly did. "Now I would like to look at your wounds." Slowly removing the bandages, Dad wet a cloth with some whiskey from his bottle and then cleaned the wounds, front and back.

Then in a few minutes, he fell asleep. Mama sat beside his bed and read from the Book.

The next day, he woke up and smiled and asked for our names. Dad and I were outside in the field taking care of the crops. Millie and Pal were there, too. Millie was hooked up to the plow, Pal was pulling a dragon, which we used to haul heavy wood and dirt like firewood, tree limbs, fence posts, and all things that were too heavy or too big for us to carry.

Mama called from the doorway, "You boys come in for a minute." Dad didn't want to stop working, but Mama needed us.

He said, "Come on, son, your mother needs us and we love her. Right, son?"

"You betcha," I said. I ran to the kitchen, grabbed Mama, and gave her a big hug. Dad came through the door and did the same.

"The man is awake and wants to know our names," she said.

"Good," Dad said. "Let's go tell him who we are."

"Glad you are feeling better," Mama said.

"I do," he replied. "My name is Nathaniel, but most people call me Nathan."

"Where are you from? Where were you born?"

"I was born in Big Gap, Georgia in the hill country. I don't really know what year." Ma and Paw were mountain people. They had a small cabin in a thicket of poplar trees. It was a good place. It was my home for many years. I thought I would never leave that beautiful place." As he spoke, his eyes became wet. "Until the night my world fell down. I think I was about twelve-years-old on that night that I will never forget." He paused as sadness took over his face. Then I sat down on the side of his bed.

He took my hand and said, "My boy, I hope that what happened to my family never happens to this family." In a moment, he started talking again.

Right after dusk, old Rover began to bark. We thought a wild animal was near the house. Old Rover was a good watchdog. Suddenly there was a pistol shot, and we heard old Rover squeal. Paw jumped to get his rifle.

He opened the door and yelled, "Who is out there?" Then two rifle shots were fired at once. The bullets hit Paw in the chest. He fell out the door into the yard. Ma grabbed me. and we headed out the kitchen door. We were a way from the house when I heard a single shot and then Ma fell. She yelled, "Run, son run."

"Not without you, Ma."

"Go, son go."

"Ma, Ma," I cried.

"Go, son go," as her voice faded away. I could hardly see, but I ran in the brush. I found a large oak tree and climbed to the top. I was shaking so hard, my body was out of control.

In a minute, I spotted two men looking for me.

One said, "We have to find that kid and get rid of him." They came closer to the tree I was in, and suddenly there they were. The moonlight hit their faces, and I could see them clearly. For a long time, they kept looking for me. Then I heard two horses coming down the trail. Soon they were out of ear shot.

I could not move. I was stuck to the tree limb. How long I was up the tree, I do not know. Finally I came down and headed for my house. First I found Ma. I sat down and put her head in my lap and stayed there for a long time. Her words, "Go, son, go," kept running through my head. The sun was peeping through the trees. Then I thought about Paw. I found him lying in the yard. Somehow I got them both into our house and put them into their bed and covered them up.

The house had been ransacked, and anything of value was gone, except Paw's guns. He had hidden them behind loose bricks in the chimney. They were still there—two pistols and two belts full of bullets. I knew I could not stay in our home any more. So I loaded my saddle bags with what food I could find, a bed roll, and some clothes. Then I saddled up our horse, Pet, and started down the trail in the same direction as the killers.

Before I left, I went back into our house, bid my Ma ad Paw goodbye, poured oil over the house and over my parent's bed, then I set it ablaze.

As I watched the house burn, I said to myself, "I will get the two men that took their lives. Now you go to your Heaven, Ma and Paw."

It did not take long for me to find those monsters. One day I watched them go into a saloon, laughing and drinking, having a good time. Anger swept over me. So I strapped on my two guns, walked down the street, and into the saloon.

As I went through the doors, I heard someone say, "Look at the kid with the big guns," and everyone started laughing.

I walked over close to the two killers, pulled out both guns, and yelled, "These two men killed my ma and paw a few days ago. I am here to kill them."

The two started laughing and said, "Boy, you can't even shoot those pistols." Everyone started to giggle. I pulled both triggers at the same time, hitting them in the stomach. I watched them slump to the floor. I stood over them and yelled again, "These two men killed my parents." I looked down at them and said, "You Satan boys are headed to hell." Then I shot them both in the head. Then I rode out of that town on Pet and a gun on each hip. I have been roaming the land for many years. I fell in love with all the beauty and open spaces. Since then I have not hurt another man or woman, in fact I have helped out a few.

Mama and Dad seemed to be speechless, but I felt he had done a good deed. I think I would have done the same if someone hurt my mama and dad.

So I said to him is a whisper, "You did good, sir."

Dan spoke, "Nathan, I believe you. I would like for you to stay here for a while. You could teach my son to shoot those pistols. He will need to know how to defend himself." Mama didn't like the idea. She was a little frightened, I think. Dad put his hand on her shoulder and pulled her close.

After a moment, she said, "Fine with me." I ran and retrieved my books about Cowboy Bill and asked Nathan if he would teach me to read them. Mama said, "Son, I have been reading them to you."

Nathan smiled at Mama and said, "Could we not both read to him and at the same time teach him to read?"

"Yes," Mama said. "Oh, by the way, my name is Ruth, Ruth Smith. Dad's name is David, David Allen. This young boy's name is Billy, Billy Allen. Our home is in Kentucky, which we left some time ago. When David and I met, we wanted our own home farther west. Our home town was getting too crowded, people everywhere. We married, bid farewell to our families, loaded up our wagon, and headed west. Our hometown of Lawrence would not miss

The Last Ride

us. We were on the trail west for many months. It was wonderful. Along the way, we made friends, ate with them, slept in their homes. All of their names are Written in the Book. Maybe someday we will see some of them again. We finally reached what we thought was Oklahoma, but we found out later that we were in Texas. We didn't care for we had found a beautiful valley with flat land and hills and no one around. Not too long after we reached our valley, I built our cabin, and soon Billy was born. Jesus has blessed us three with the fruits of the land. But first, Nathan, tell us how and why you were shot. It had to be with a rifle."

"Yes, I am lucky to be here. God's plan, I guess. I was in Tylertown getting some salt, pork, and beans when three rough looking men came in; for what, I don't know. They had been drinking. One of them knocked over a piece goods table, Bible and the madam, the owner's wife, asked them to pick up the piece goods and put them back on the table.

She said, 'Put them back on the table, and do it now,' raising her voice a tone or two.

One of the cowboys grabbed her by the arm and said, 'Lady, don't you talk to me like that. You pick them up, lady. I don't take orders from a woman.' The other two just laughed. The owner was headed for his gun.

One of them yelled at him and said, 'Stop.' The situation was getting out of hand, so to speak. I was caught in the middle of it all. The madam was then slapped twice.

So I spoke up and said, 'I wouldn't do that again if I were you,' hoping that all would quiet down. Well it didn't. I was the focus now of their anger. I pulled both guns out of my holsters and quietly said, 'I think you three better leave.'

They left, but one turned around and said, 'We will get you for this.' We watched them until they went into the saloon. I knew I was in trouble—three drunken cowboys getting drunker. I got my supplies, put them on my horse, and looked around. The dry goods owner didn't charge me for my supplies. The madam thanked me over and over. Now the drunkards were not mad at the store owner, they were mad at me. Although I helped them, I was the one they would be after. Not seeing anyone, I thought I could make it out of town before they knew I was gone. They must have been watching for me to exit the dry goods store. All of a sudden, I had three drunk men chasing me. I did have a little head start in hopes that I could make it to the trees before they could shoot me. I almost made it. One of their shots hit me. I slumped in my saddle but did not fall off my horse. I believe they thought I was finished because they stopped following me. Somehow I found the trail that brought me to your house. Pet just kept going. When you found me, I could barely see. Thank you again, my friends."

Nathan looked at Mama and said, "Would you please bring me your bible?" When she gave it to him, he placed his hand on it, closed his eyes, saying, "Thank you, Jesus, for saving me. I owe you one, my Lord." That day Nathan became almost like one of our family. We were all happy about it. At first he slept on some hay grass. The weather was warm, and I think he liked it out there.

Dad said, "We have to build you a room on the back of our house. We will start tomorrow, finding the logs. On top of all that, we need an additional stall in the barn." Another cow was born. We needed a larger fence.

However, Nathan would find time to read to me and teach me the words. He and Dad and Mama would watch me shoot the pistols. With words and instructions from Nathan, how lucky I was to be a boy on a farm with people that loved me.

As the years went by, I learned to read; Dad brought home more books. All were mostly about cowboys and the deeds they were doing to save the west from outlaws. As I read more and more, I pictured myself as a cowboy hero. I practiced my draw every day. Soon my arm muscles grew stronger. Faster and faster was my draw, and I could hit what I was shooting at. My desire to be a cowboy and go out west was mostly what I thought about. It became my dream.

One morning, just after sun came up, I walked out to the barn to count the cows and water the horses, Pet, Pal, and Millie the mule. I would take them one at the time to the spring house to let them drink. I always would take Pal first. She was a beautiful mare. This morning she was nervous. I tried to settle her down, but I couldn't. All of a sudden, she snatched the rope out of my hand and ran into the woods.

"Dad, Dad, come quick." I guess my voice sounded urgent. Out the house door came both Dad and Nathan.

The Last Ride

"What is up, son?" yelled Dad.

"Pal has run away. She seemed nervous this morning and she pulled the rope out of my hand and ran off."

"We will go find her. I am sure she won't go very far."

"I don't know, Dad," I said, "she was running hard."

"Which way did she go, son?"

"Out through the field that way."

Nathan said, "I will go find her."

Dad said, "I will go, too. Son, you stay with your mama." Dad put a bridle on Millie and crawled on her back. We had no saddle for Millie. Nathan put his saddle on Pet and also put a bridle on her head. The two headed off in the direction that Pal had taken.

Nathan had taken the lead. His horse was faster than Millie.

They must have searched for hours when Dad said to Nathan, "It's time to go home before we get lost."

Nathan said, "Let's dismount and rest a while." They were sitting on tree roots, not making a sound. Out of nowhere came the sound of hoof beats. Out of the trees came two horses. Pal was one of them. The other was a stallion that looked almost like Pal.

"Well," said Dad, "now we know why she ran away." They watched the stallion perform his duty. After that they ran side by side for a short distance, the stallion stopped, reared upon his hind legs, let out a loud whinny, turned, and ran away. Pal made a circle like she wanted to follow, but she didn't. She turned and headed home.

Nathan said, "Let her go home her way." When Dad and Nathan got home, Billy was already with Pal. I guess he had stayed at the barn waiting for Pal to return. He was hugging her and talking to her.

Mama yelled from the kitchen door, "You men come in now. It's time to eat your breakfast, or I guess I should say your dinner."

A few months later, Dad said, "Son, Pal is pregnant with a baby. Do you know what that means?"

"Yes," I said. Then it hit me, this baby will become my horse. I kept that thought to myself.

Something was always disturbing the cattle and upsetting the horses. We had to keep our guns handy, so we could grab them and run out to find out what was bothering the animals. As soon as we open the kitchen door, you would hear them running through the brush. Sometimes one of us would take a pot shot at something hopefully that would keep them from coming back again.

Until one night after a shot fired after an animal, someone in the dark cried out, "Don't shoot, it's just me."

"Who is me?" Nathan cried out.

"It's me, Uncle Ned." We all cranked our guns. Dad and Nathan got behind a tree and a fence post. Not me, I stood in place with my two pistols cocked. If I was going to be a hero of the west, I had to stand my ground, I thought.

Dad reached over and pulled me over behind him, saying, "Son, don't make yourself a target. Let's find out who this is first. All right, Uncle Ned, show yourself." Not a movement from Uncle Ned. Nathan raised his rifle. All was quiet. It was pretty dark also. Then a figure of a man was slowly walking toward us. "Keep coming," Dad yelled. As he got close enough for us to see that he had no guns, we put ours away.

His first words were, "Could you spare a bite to eat? I don't remember when I ate last, and may I drink some water out of the horse's bucket?" With that he stumbled and fell toward me. I caught him and tried to hold him up. He sit down by this tree root. Nathan got him some water. Dad headed to the kitchen to get him some food. He came back soon with biscuits and honey. Uncle Ned grabbed at the biscuits. But Dad held back.

"Now, Uncle Ned, go slowly. You don't want to make yourself sick." Mama came out with a glass of milk. She had been watching from the kitchen door. All was quiet except for Uncle Ned. He was chomping on biscuits and licking honey. He was so happy, I could not help it. I shed a tear.

To our surprise, Uncle Ned put his hand in his coat pocket. Dad said, "What have you got in that pocket?" Dad laid his hand on his arm. Slowly Uncle Ned pulled out a new born puppy. He handed it to me.

"Would you get him some milk?" The puppy looked into my eyes as to say please. He made a slight whimpering sound and seemed to relax in my arms.

Mama said, "He is too young to drink out of a saucer, but I have just the thing you need to feed him with." She returned with a baby bottle with a nipple attached. "This was your bottle when you were born. I saved it to remind me of the time I held you and fed you when you were a little baby. Now you can use it to feed another baby. That little puppy needs to be cared for."

"Yes, Mama." I poured some milk into the bottle, held the puppy in my arms, and let some milk drop around his mouth. At first he didn't know how to suck the nipple. So I held open his mouth just enough to let some milk enter his mouth. Then he knew what to do. After feeding for a while, he went to sleep in my arms. Mama got an old sack and placed it behind the cook stove.

"Son, go lay him on the sack. He needs to rest."

Then Dad came in from outside. He asked Mama if it was okay to bring Uncle Ned into the kitchen. Of course Mama said he could. Dad considers the house Mama's property. Nathan came in with Uncle Ned and sat him down in a kitchen chair.

He said, "Ma, could I have another biscuit and maybe a little more milk?" which he consumed quickly.

Dad said, "You need to be cleaned up, Ned, and you probably need to sleep."

"Yes, sir, I do."

"Nathan, would you show him where the water hole is and show him where he can sleep tonight? Show him where you slept before we built a room for you."

"Sure," Nathan responded.

"Hold on," Dad said. "Let me get a pair of my old long johns. Ned, you wash yourself and wash your clothes. Nathan will show you where you may sleep. Sleep in the long johns. While you rest, hang your clothes on the fence to dry overnight."

The next morning, I slept later than usual. Then I ran into the kitchen to see the new puppy. He wasn't there.

"Mama," I cried, "where is my puppy?"

"Nathan took him outside. I think he missed his old dog Rover, the dog that the two drunks killed the night they also shot his ma and paw. Don't go outside just yet. Let him stay with Nathan a little longer. It might help him forget that awful night. Here, son, eat your breakfast."

"Thanks, Mama." I ate my breakfast kinda fast so I could go outside. "May I go now, Mama?"

"Yes, son," she said with a smile. I ran outside and found Nathan and Uncle Ned sitting on some tree roots. Uncle Ned was holding the puppy. After all it was his puppy. I sat down on a root between them. The puppy looked at him and gave out a yelp. Uncle Ned handed him to me. He yelped again as I held him in my lap. Nathan looked over at Uncle Ned.

"Yes," he said with a grin. Dad walked up about that time and looked at me holding the dog.

"How do you like your dog, son?"

"What?" I said in amazement.

"Uncle Ned wanted you to have him."

"My dog, my dog. Thank you, Uncle Ned. I will take good care of him."

"I know you will," Ned replied.

"What do you want to call him?" Nathan asked.

"I don't know." I was speechless. Then Nathan spoke up.

"I have a name you might like."

"What is it?" I asked.

"You know my dog that I had when I was about your age, I named him Rover. What about you calling him Rover." It didn't take me long to say yes.

I looked down at my dog and said, "Hello, Rover." He yelped his approval, or it sounded like he approved.

"Ned," I asked, "what happened to Rover?"

"Well, son, she was just an old hound dog, but she and I were partners for a long time. She was black with white spots on her face, a pretty thing to me. One day we decided to travel, leave home and explore this country. And that is exactly what we did. We walked a lot of miles together. The night I made it here, she was too tired and too old to continue our journey. She lay down beside me and gave birth to three puppies. Rover here is the only one that lived. After the birth, she went back to sleep and never woke up. She just could not go any farther. Son, Rover here is what she gave her life for."

The Last Ride

Dad spoke up and said, "Let's all go into the kitchen. I want Uncle Ned to tell us all about him and where he came from."

Ned spoke, "No, you all don't need to hear about me or where I came from. My life has been kind of useless, very dull."

"No, Ned, we all want to know. You can be someone that stays here. I have to know about your life before you got here and how you ended up with us."

"I am not from around here. My home is far away, that way." Then he became very quiet as tears fell from his eyes. He choked and could not speak. When he was able to say something, he spoke with quivering lips. "I am from Georgia, near Atlanta. You all heard about Atlanta, Georgia, haven't you?" Dad nodded a yes. "Do you know that they grow a lot of cotton in Georgia? Please don't get upset for I am going to tell you the truth. I was a slave on Mr. Patrick Bellow's plantation for many years until the day Mr. Bellows passed away. After he died, his son took over his father's duties. In a few months, everything changed. The son let his new authority go wild. He started to whip us if we did not work as hard or as long as he thought we should. We had to watch as he took a bullwhip and lashed one of us until they died. He even set the dogs on one of us, and they mauled him till he died. That was his way, I guess, of staying in control. Many of our children were sold to other plantations, some as far away as New York. We never saw them again. I don't know where my son and daughter are today. I hope they are still alive. My wife of a long time came down sick with grief. She died from a broken heart. She stopped eating and passed away. I felt that I was all alone on the plantation. My dreams were so bad that I could not sleep. I thought I had rather be dead than live like I am forced to on this plantation. I began to black out time after time. After a year or so, my mind was made up. I am leaving this place. All I ever had was gone from me now. I was alone and full of anger. But the anger was probably keeping me alive.

I thought of ways to kill Mr. Bellow's son, whose name was Joseph. Mr. Joseph has to die was always on my mind. Then I thought, if I kill Mr. Joseph, I would surely hang. So I decided to run away. That might be my only chance for freedom. How foolish can a man be, I thought. It would be better to die a free man than a slave man. One night a foreman got very drunk and misplaced his rifle. I saw where he placed it in the bushes. I stole it late that night and hid it in a potato hill. When Mr. Joseph heard that he had lost his rifle, the foreman quit his job and left the plantation but not before Mr. Joseph threatened to shoot him.

One night when most of his slaves were outside around a fire, playing music and dancing, I went to the horse barn. All the noise kept the dogs at bay. I put a saddle on the best horse, got the rifle out of the potato hill, and quietly walked across the field into the trail in the woods. Then I mounted my horse and rode away from the plantation. Over about the last four or five weeks or more, I am not sure, or four or five months, I traveled at night, following the sky.

One day this stray dog found me. I fed him some fish. Then he never left until last night. My horse just fell down and couldn't get up. About then I was thinking I would be next. I kept walking every night until the night I saw your lights. If I was going to die, I was ready. You now know that I am a runaway slave with no place to call home. Now that I have told you my life story, I will keep walking following the sky, but I would really like to stay here for a while."

I spoke up and said, "Sure, you can stay here."

Dad interrupted me, "Hold on, son. We will all have to make this decision together." Nathan spoke up, "It could be dangerous to harbor a runaway slave if they found him here. We could be harmed, and they would kill Ned." Dad and Ma said the right thing to do is to let him stay, and of course I wanted him to stay. So Ned stayed on our ranch. We built him a room beside Nathan's on the back of the house. Over time our cows had other cows and one of them was a male, which made Dad happy. Our ranch grew larger. We put up barbed wire to keep the cows from going too far away. I kept reading whatever book I could find in town, practicing my draw and shooting. But I was getting restless. I wanted to be more like Cowboy Bill. I would re-read his book and dream of places I would like to visit. I was fourteen now and a man. I felt it was time for me to leave my home. After all Dad and Ma have Nathan and Ned to help with the garden, Millie, Pal, Pet, and the cows.

When I told Mama and Dad my plans, they both said, "No, son, you are too young. Let's wait a few more years."

"No, it's time," I replied. "I want to be like Cowboy Bill."

"But son," Mama expressed, "they are only stories. The country will not be like what you are reading about."

"I want to see for myself what is out there. You know how I like to explore the woods and creeks around our home. It's like someone is whispering in my ear – go find your place in this big land."

"Son, you are a dreamer and you have many skills to help you on your way. You are as big as your father, but your heart is so big. Please listen to Jesus. He will tell you if it is time. You know you will be missed by your parents but also by Nathan and Ned."

"Yes, Mama, I will miss them, too." Dad had not said a word. He walked outside with tears in his eyes. Mama followed him out the door. She clasped his hand and then they walked slowly down the road.

I did not sleep well that night. My mind was already away from here, dreaming of places far away. I heard Mama crying next door, which made me very sad.

The next morning, the weather was pouring down rain and there was a chill in the air. I went to the barn to see Nathan and Ned. Because of the rain, they had found a dry spot in the hay weeds.

Ned spoke first, "Billy, your dad told us that you were leaving home for places unknown. Let me tell you about those places unknown. It's not like you think, and it is not like stories in books. You may not survive. I thought I was going to die several times as I traveled to here. But by the grace of Jesus, I lived. I think I would like to go with you. Maybe between the two of us, we might make it."

"No, Ned," I said, "Dad needs you here."

"Nathan has already said that he would go into town and find two poor cowboys that needed a home."

Nathan spoke up, "I have two in mind now. They work some at the stables, and I believe they would like it here on your dad's ranch. You see, Billy, we have it all figured out. But we know you will have to ask your Lord if it will be the right way to go. Ned will need a horse and saddle. We have decided that he will take Pet as his horse. I will give him papers to show that I gave him my horse, Pet. Billy, you have your horse, Pal Junior. I know where I can get a new horse to replace Pet. If your dad approves, we will be lucky." I could not leave that day; I must wait for Nathan to go to town and bring back a horse and two wranglers. I wanted to go with him because I wanted to look over the two cowboys and see if he could obtain a horse also. The rain had slowed up, which made it easier to travel to town. Ned stayed with Dad and Mama. Nathan or Ned was always nearby when Mama was at home.

We reached town before noon and went directly to the livery stables. Two hands were currying two horses that belonged to a couple of riders that arrived about early morning. One of the hands told us that they went over to the saloon to get some breakfast. They sure have beautiful horses, I thought as I touched one of their noses. Nathan got into a session with the two stable hands. They all seemed to be happy with what was being paid. Soon they came back into the barn.

Nathan came over and said, "What do you think?" pointing over to the stable hands.

"Do they have a horse?" I asked.

"See those two ponies in the last stall? They belong to them." I went over to take a look at the young horses, Pintos, and on the rails were two saddles. So they agree to go work on Dad's ranch. Yes, but I have to give the hard facts and get some answers from them. I will do that when we get back to the ranch.

"Mister," one of the hands said to Nathan. "Let me show you a horse that was left here about two months ago. The man that left him here never came back for him. I guess he died or something happened to him." This got Nathan's attention. He looked over the horse and rubbed his neck. It was like they liked each other. Nathan looked for a branch, but there was none. He thought to himself, this horse was wild but tamed by the man that left him here. His saddle was on the rail.

The owner of the stables and barn came down from the loft. He had heard and saw all that had been going on.

"If you two want to go work on a ranch, you have my permission. There is not much left for you here. I will find someone else to tend the horses."

The Last Ride

Nathan replied, "Thank you, sir."

"Mr. Jones is my name. They call me Sid."

"Mister Sid, that horse in that stall needs to get out and run for a while." Nathan asked, "If you let me take him to our ranch, I will care for her until the owner shows up, and if he does, you know where she will be." Sid thought for a while.

"Okay," he said, "all she is doing here is eating a lot of my hay. Saddle her up, fellows, and your ponies, too."

"Sid, I will leave a paper to show to the owner of the horse if he comes back. We will be at the Smith-Allen Ranch about twenty miles west." Two cowboys laughing and talking came through the barn door.

One of them said, "Boy, why aren't you currying my horse?"

"I already did that, sir. Your horse is ready for you."

"Don't look like it to me!" The cowboy yelled.

"Now saddle him up for me, and the other one, too."

"Yes, sir," was the reply. The two stable hands put the blankets on each horse and then the saddles. "Your horses are ready, sirs." The two hands were pushed aside as the two cowboys mounted their horses.

The owner of the barn said, "Excuse me, gentlemen, you owe me two bits a horse. That will be four bits for their care."

With a loud voice came, "I am not paying you a penny. Your work was shoddy."

Billy stepped in front of the horses and said, "I think you two should pay your debt."

"I am not paying anyone anything," was shouted to Billy.

"Sir," Billy said, "because you refused to pay two bits a horse, the price has now gone up to four bits a horse. Now pay up, or we will keep the horses till you do."

"Kid, you can't tell me what to do."

Billy replied, "I just did." One of them let his hand fall to his gun. Nathan stepped in.

"I would not do that if I were you, sir."

"Are you afraid that this young one will get hurt?"

"No, sir, I am afraid you will get hurt. I would recommend that you pay the four bits a horse and be on your way."

"Get out of my way, boy."

"Billy is my name, and you are not going anywhere until you pay your debt."

The two cowboys looked at Billy and then at each other. Then one said, "I think we better pay." He handed the owner eight bits.

"Thank you," said the owner as the cowboys rode out of the livery stables. No one said a word as we saddled our horses. Nathan gave the owner a piece of paper and thanked him for his courtesy. I was aboard Pal Junior, Nathan was aboard his new mare, the two stable hands were on their pintos, and Pet was following behind.

I decided not to leave until a few days later. Ned and I would like to observe how the two new cowpokes were working out. Dad said he believed they would be good workers. Mama had been quiet for a while since I announced I was leaving home to go to the west. Nathan was the foreman. He liked it. The herd of cows was growing, so he asked Dad if it would be appropriate to scout out more land. We will need more grazing land. He and Dad were planning a layout of the surrounding areas and put up posted signs and let all know that the land belonged to the Allen-Smith Ranch.

That night Ned and I made plans to leave the next day. We both felt good about this decision. The ranch was in good hands now, and Dad and Mama had got used to the idea of me leaving the ranch.

So in the morning, it was time I said my goodbyes. At breakfast was a good time. Mama started crying. Dad did a little of the same.

He spoke up, looking at Mama with a broken voice, "Mama," he said, "think back when we were young. We did the same thing years ago. We followed our dream. Heading west was all we could think about. Now it's his dream. Ruth, he has my blessing, and he would like yours also, Mama." She got up and left the table.

I went outside to the stables where Ned was. Pal was already saddled. He was just waiting for me. I bridled Pal Junior and put the saddle on over his blanket, put on my two pistols, and climbed aboard. Nathan and the two new cowpokes also were there.

Dad and Mama came out of the house and in unison said, "We love you, son." Then Mama said, "You have my blessing."

Dad gave me a rifle, saying, "You will need this to kill you some food." Ned and I told our goodbyes. Off we went down the trail. I stopped to look back and saw Mama in the doorway, crying with a Bible in her hand.

The first few days on the trail were easy. I thought to myself, *I have done the right thing*. My heart was full of happiness. Ned and I were enjoying the beauty of all we saw. I think Ned enjoyed it more than I did. He was probably thinking about the days he was a slave and now he is a free man.

That night I asked him, "Ned, tell me about your wife and children. Do you think you will ever see them again?" He didn't answer. He just kindly looked at me with sad eyes. I said no more. Then he spoke.

"Billy, have you ever thought about how your mom and pop would feel if someone were to take you away from them?"

"What was your wife's name?" At first he could not speak. So I said no more. Then he spoke again.

"Thelma was her name. I loved her very much. She may be gone forever." Sadness crept over me. I looked up and saw Heaven and the face of God smiling at me.

Rover was always by my side. Somehow he knew we were in a wilderness and he was the lookout. I knew he would alert us if anything or anyone came near our camp. Our food was always a rabbit, a deer, even a rattler. Our fire was started by two pieces of flint, which worked most of the time. Ned had a bag of black powder. With the flint and black powder and some dry leaves and twigs, it was easy to start a fire. The weather was not our friend. A lot of the days and nights were filled with high winds and rain showers.

In the day time, we traveled west by the sun and at night by the stars. When the days or nights were without sun or stars, we gave it our best guess. Our food was fish when we could catch them. Most of the meat was from animals that came too close to our camp. We tried not to waste any food. Most of the time we would cook it over an open fire and then pack it in a dry skin pouch. It could last for days. No one ever came our way, but we were not lonely for we had our freedom to be ourselves with a background of beauty. Sometimes late at night our families and home would cause us to reminisce about what we had left behind.

A short time later, when we were in hilly county on the crest of a hill, or maybe a mountain, our horses were feeding on the grass. Our bodies were at rest as we observed a beautiful valley. It must have been about mid-summer. I was about half asleep when Ned punched me.

"Wake up, Billy. Look over to your right. Tell me what you see."

"Nothing, Ned."

"Look harder, Billy." Then I saw what he was looking at. A puff of smoke and then a building.

"Ned, someone must be living down there. Should we go visit?"

"I don't know," Ned replied. "Could be dangerous. It's too hot for a fire. They must be cooking." Then the thought of food took over our minds.

I said, "Let's go knock on their door." The horses had about finished eating the tall grass. Now they needed water. There has to be a stream somewhere down in a low spot, probably close to the cabin.

"Let's go," Ned said. The hill was a little steep, so we didn't mount then. It was best to walk and lead the horses. It took us longer to get down the hill than I thought it would be. Things look a lot closer than they actually are.

We approached the cabin but did not see or hear anything or anyone. Ned started to lower his rifle.

"No, Ned, we must not appear hostile."

"You're right, Billy. Let's stay calm with our eyes and ears open."

"Hello in the cabin," I called pretty loud.

A man walked out of the door and asked, "Are you here to help?" His face showed desperation.

Ned whispered, "Tell him we will try."

"Yes," was my answer.

"Come on in," he said. Then we heard the click of a rifle as a boy came around the corner of the cabin. We both didn't move, and they didn't say a word. Rover let out a growl. I placed my hand on him and patted his head.

The Last Ride

"It's okay, boy."

"Are you really here to help? Where did you come from?"

"From the hills of north Texas. My dad was a rancher there. I left because I wanted to see more of the west. This is my friend, Ned. We are here to help if we can." He lowered his gun, but he didn't put it down.

"Okay, Pa, let them in and take a look at Ma." Inside there was a woman lying on a cot with a leg that was very swollen.

The old man said, "She had been down to the creek to get a bucket of water when she met a porcupine. When she tried to run, the animal stuck her leg with sharp bones."

Ned said, "He means quills."

"Pa took them all out, but her leg does not get well. In fact it gets worse every day; I think it is the devil making Ma sick."

Ned whispered, "Probably some of those quills are still in her leg."

"I agree. We will have to get them out, or she might die. Her leg is showing a bad infection. We have to dig them out now."

"Billy, you explain what has to be done, or she might die."

Pa said, "What is your name, son?"

"Pa and Ma call me Sunrise."

"Why are you called by that name?"

"Because Ma said when I was born, the sun started shining on me through the window and that it was a sign from the spirits that I was special. Pa said he delivered me, and I was special. The spirits will always be with you." More about that later, I thought. "Get me some hot water and stick that poker in the hot ashes. Try to get it red hot. I will need some pieces of cloth to make a bandage to cover the wound. Sunrise, will you help?"

"Yes, Billy, I will."

"Get me the sharpest knife you have. If it is not sharp, sharpen it."

"I will get the knife." All was soon ready.

"Now Sunrise, you and Pa go wait outside. Ma will scream some. Let me explain what I have to do." Which I did. Ned was leery. I said, "We have no choice. She will die soon if we don't try, and Sunrise may kill us if she dies." We were in a no-win situation. He placed his body across her waist and put his hands on her shoulder. I sat on her feet and tried to keep her still. This was going to hurt her.

Billy took the knife to the wound. She let out a scream so loud, louder than I had ever heard before. To our good luck, she fainted, which was a blessing. I dug down into the wound and then I saw the quills. One, two, three. I got them out, took the knife, and scraped the wound till I thought it was clean of infected tissue.

"Ned," I said, "hand me the hot rod." He did, and I laid the rod in the wound until all the red tissue was now black. Ma was still passed out. Lucky me. "Heat the rod again, Ned. I may need it to check for any places I may have missed." After close inspection, I decided that the wound was clean. I then pulled the wound together and wrapped her leg with the rags.

"Ned, get some cool water and wash her face. She needs to wake up now." A few minutes later, she opened her eyes. It's time to let Pa and Sunrise see Ma. I yelled, "Pa, you can come see Ma now."

"Billy, we should get going now. She may not live, and Sunrise might shoot us."

"She will live, the spirit is in her."

"Are you sure, Billy?"

We will not run away. We will see it through. She will get well. I will pray to my Lord Jesus Christ."

Pa and Sunrise came back in, and Ma smiled but did not say a word. I told Pa to fix her some soup or beans. I think she will be fine in a few days. Ned and I were preparing to leave when Sunrise suggested that we stay for a while. A few days, we could help cut firewood for the cold day and nights. Pa usually would help, but now he is too old to cut trees. Pa was busy hanging some deer meat over the fire.

He said, "You boys hungry, I bet."

"Yes we could stand to sleep inside a cabin and eat someone else's cooking." I was a bit leery of staying at all. If Ma didn't get better, we could be in danger. Ned was eyeing the cooking deer meat.

Sunrise spoke up, "You can sleep here on the floor. It's where I sleep."

Sometime later, as it was getting dark outside as we finished our supper, I asked Sunrise how they came to live in such a beautiful valley.

The Last Ride

Pa interrupted, "Years ago I was going west, kind of like what you two are doing. But I was alone. You two know how this wilderness seems to take control of you and won't let go. You just want to see what is over the next hill. I am from St. Louis. Perhaps you have heard of St. Louis."

"Yes, I have heard of such a town."

"I spent several months just me and a mule and a horse. As you can see, there are three horses inside the fence out back. They are new, somewhat. Sunrise and I caught them ourselves. They were wild and dangerous when we caught them. Our old mule and old horse died. But the spirit has brought us more horses." He looked over at Ma and said, "Don't you worry, Ma, the spirit will make you better," and he smiled at her as a tear fell from his eye.

"I started west with happy hopes and a love for freedom–freedom from people and town noise. After a long, long journey through the woods and streams, bears, and most everything else, one day I saw a lot of Indians on a hill, so I ran and hid in some brush. I forgot about my horse and left him tied to a tree along with my mule. I ran back out to get them, so I could hide them also behind me in the trees. I felt safe then, but I was wrong. They had already seen me, I guess. They came off the hill and took me to their camp. As you can see, they didn't kill me. They let me stay and live with them for about two years, more or less.

Ma here is an Apache woman. We fell in love after about one year after I started living as an Apache. We were an Apache wedding way. The days and nights were good to us until the soldiers came and raided and killed most of the tribe. It was the saddest day of our lives. Ma and I were walking down by a lake's stream, leading our horses. Kinda courting, I guess. When we saw ahead all the screaming and shooting, we mounted our horses and rode across the stream and over the hills. No soldier had followed us. The next morning, we rode back to our home and found many bodies slaughtered. Family members dead."

Ma had listened as he told his story and she wept. So did Pa. So did Ned and I. After a long silence, Pa started his life's story again.

"I built this cabin about twenty years ago, I think. We have been here ever since. I lost my yen for going farther west." He looked over at Ma and said,

"Ma is the reason why. When Sunrise was born, my life was complete. The outside world doesn't like a white man that is married to an Indian woman."

"Same way when a white man marries an African woman," I said. "The world is full of a lot of dumb people. They have never learned how to love."

Ned and I stayed with Ma, Pa, and Sunrise until Ma was able to walk pretty well. We were planning to continue our trek west soon. I was helping Sunrise with his shooting. He was very good. He had an old .45. Pa had a rifle for their protection from wolves, bears, and many more wild things that roamed the woods both day and night.

Early one morning, Ma went to the stream to get a bucket of water. Pa woke up when she opened the door.

He called, "Let me go, Ma."

"No," she replied, "it's time I start using this limp leg."

"Okay," Pa said. He watched her limp down to the stream. From out of nowhere came a pack of wolves. Pa saw them and yelled at Ma, "Wolves, run, Ma." She looked up, and the wolves were coming fast. Ma tried to run, but she couldn't because of her weak leg. Pa ran out to help her get back inside to safety. He reached her, and they started toward the cabin.

Sunrise, Ned and I grabbed our rifles and rushed outside. By then the wolves had each one by their throats. We killed three wolves as we all ran to help. The rest of the pack ran off. Sunrise picked up his ma and carried her inside and laid her on her bed. He knew she was dead. Her throat was open and bleeding. Tears flooded like rain. We laid Pa down beside her. I knew he was dead, too. Wolves attack the throat first.

Sunrise just sat in a chair beside the bed. He had no movement. I think he was in a coma. But his eyes kept dropping tears.

After a while, Sunrise stood and walked outside, looked up and yelled, "Oh, Great Spirit, where are you, and why did you take my ma and pa." Then he fell to his knees and wept.

Ned said, "Let's pack our food, take our weapons and horses."

I spoke up, "We have to bury Ma and Pa first."

Sunrise said, "No, I will. Leave them where they lie." We knew what he meant. He was going to burn down the cabin. We all got busy packing and feeding and watering the horses. About noon we were ready to start on our journey. Sunrise went into the house. I could hear him pouring oil over the floors and probably over the bed. Ned and I went into the cabin. We listened to Sunrise say his goodbyes.

He looked up and said, "Great Spirit, I am sending you my ma and pa. Take care of them." Then he set the oil on fire. We all walked to our horses, mounted them, and rode to the crest of the hill. We turned and watched the cabin go up in flames. Rover was by my side.

I looked down at him and said, "Are you ready to travel, my friend?" His tail wagged a yes. I looked up and said, "This way, gents." We were not in a hurry. Our goal was to hunt, fish, camp where we found a good place, maybe by a river or stream. There was no set time to start or stop. The weather at times would stop us for a day or two. I didn't mind that at all. When it rained, it was hard to find dry logs for the fires. We had a lot of fur pelts to trade for a home cooked meal or for some bullets. I wanted to see the Pacific Ocean. I was told that you could not see across it to the other side. If we kept going west, I hope we would run into it.

Winter was coming on soon. We decided to head south to avoid the snow and ice. As we traveled southward, we came upon mountains that looked like big rocks with trees growing around them. The scene was so beautiful. We found a ridge that we could get up with our horses.

We said, "Let's camp here for a few days."

"Okay," said Ned. Sunrise was hesitant.

He said, "This is buffalo and wolf country I believe. Let's be on the lookout for wolves. Buffaloes can't get up on this ridge. But wolves can."

Ned said, "Rover will alert us if they come around." Three days later, we packed up and left the plateau heading more or less south, or maybe it was southeast because of the high mountains. We came upon a mountain of white sand. I thought, *Was this once an ocean beach?* Only it wasn't a mountain, just hills.

One day I rode under what looked like a large wire. None of us had ever seen anything like it. We turned back west to see where it would take us. The wire was attached to poles with glass holders. The wire had no end. It went on and on. Finally it led us to a small town. A sign on the outside of the city read, "Cedar City—A Friendly Place." We rode down the main street. All was quiet. None of us knew what day of the week it was. All days were alike to us. There were three saloons that we counted, a livery stable, and a building that had a sign that read, "We Buy Furs!"

We decided to stop and see if there was a home cooked meal to be had. It was getting late in the day, and the clouds were getting darker. A room with a bed would feel nice for a change. Although I had slept on the ground so much, I might have to sleep on the floor. Not many people were on the street. I did stop one man and ask where everyone is and what day is this.

He smiled, "Most everyone is at church. Today is Sunday. You guys been on the trail very long?"

"Yes, sir. How long, we don't know."

"I own the livery stable down the street. If you are going to be here a while, let me stable your horses."

"We would, sir, but we don't have any money."

"That is all right, you can pay me with a fur. Tomorrow old Mr. Jones will buy all your furs if he likes you. He is also the church Pastor. Take your horses down to the stable. You can get a fine supper at Aunt Bell's Saloon."

A little later, we entered Aunt Bell's. She was a bit older than I was—probably at least fifty. There we all three stood: Ned, Sunrise, and Billy. Not a pretty sight for we hadn't bathed in a while and never shaved.

"Are you Aunt Bell?"

"Yes," was her response.

"We are looking for some supper, but we don't have any money until we sell our furs tomorrow."

"Do I have your word you will pay me tomorrow?"

Billy spoke up, "Yes, ma'am, you have my word."

She said, "Around here a man's word is his bond. Go back there and take a bath, then cut off some of that ugly beard. A bath costs ten cents."

Later, all cleaned up, we three walked back into the saloon. It was crowded with more folks. We all had our guns on. You don't know what to expect, so we are always ready for what may come. The saloon got very quiet.

"Aunt Bell, we each would like a steak and water."

"A beer comes with the steak."

"Just some water please."

"Where you boys from?" someone asked.

"Well," I said, "back east."

Another voice came out of the crowd, "I don't think we should allow half breeds and black men and anyone that they associate with stay in this town. Why don't you three hightail it out of town?"

I whispered to Ned and Sunrise, "Move away." They moved away from Billy about ten feet. Then Billy asked, "Who is doing this talking?" Then a big man stood, two guns on his hips.

Billy said, "Sir, let me introduce us to you and your friends. My name is Mister Bill, and this black man is Uncle Ned, and this is Sunrise," I said. "Sir, I see you are a Satan man. Are you ready to join him in Hell?" My eyes turned dark blue and I lowered my hand. He turned and walked out the door.

Just then when Billy said, "Honor," a bolt of lightning struck a tree nearby, and the charge went through them all. Billy looked at the man.

"I think Jesus has spoken. Give him back his guns. Now get on your horse and go home. Get back to your ranch, hug your wife and kids."

"Billy, are you sure you want to let him go? He may come after us later. We can't kill him for then we will be punished."

"Let him go. Let's hope his ranch will grow and the town people will respect him, and most of all, may he learn to love his family as we love ours or loved ours. What is your name?" I asked.

"Clyde Tucker."

"Now get going." Rover never made a sound. He just sat there looking like a happy dog. We watched as he left. He stopped and looked back at us. Then he gave a wave and headed home.

"It's getting late," Sunrise said as he felt all the rain bounce off his cowboy hat. He loved that old hat. Probably because it was his only hat. "We need to find a shelter for the night. There looks like something over behind the trees."

"Okay, let's give it a try," echoed Ned. The three did find a shallow hole or cave to camp for the night. By morning the rain had stopped.

They found the wire on the poles and headed west following the wire. All went well for the next week or so. They didn't keep time or days.

Billy said, "It didn't matter, but the heat and the cold weather, that it did." It was easy to keep up with the seasons. Just watch the sun.

One night as we were bedding down, Sunrise asked, "Do you hear that?"

"What?" Ned asked.

"It sounds like people are laughing and singing." We all stopped and opened our ears. "Someone is having a hoe-down."

It was hot the next morning, and they soon found out why. They came up to a sea of sand.

Billy said, "Do you think we should walk across and see what is on the other side?"

Ned laughed and said, "There may not be another side. It sounds like there are a lot of people that way."

"Well let's go see. It's getting darker now. Let's bed down for the night." Sometime about midnight, Rover put out a growl and he nudged me to wake me up. I saw that his tail was between his hind legs. That meant someone or something was nearby. I laid my hand on him and picked up my rifle at the same time. My eyes followed Rover's, but I didn't see any movement in the tall brushes and trees. Rover's ears stood straight up. His growl got a little louder.

"Stay, boy," I said quietly. I leaned back against a tree and covered my face with my sleeve. Ned and Sunrise looked like they were still asleep.

Out from behind the bushes stepped two baby wolves. They looked hungry. Something must have happened to their mother. I quickly reached into my food supply and pulled out a piece of deer meat.

"Stay, Rover," I said. Then I sat down on the grass and laid the meat between my knees. To my surprise, they came slowly for the food. As they ate, I placed my legs and cuddled them with my pants legs. I think I fell in love with them, too. I took leather straps from my saddle and slowly tied it around their neck, tying the other end to my belt buckle. *What am I doing?* I thought.

What am I doing? I thought. The pack could be near. "Rover, it's all right." He wagged his tail and laid down. "Good boy." Then I gave him a meat

The Last Ride

treat. In a short time, I must have fallen asleep. When I awoke, Ned and Sunrise were standing over me. They both asked, "Where did you get those babies?" Then I realized the wolves were asleep and lying on my chest. I think they were listening to my heart beat. Rover was watching them as he probably did all night.

While Sunrise and Ned were getting some meat from the bags on the pack horse, I took things out of my saddle bags and placed them in a bag on the pack horse. We all ate—Rover and the wolves also. I had to chew some meat and then feed it to the pups as I did last night. When we were ready to break camp, I placed each wolf in my saddle bag and tied the string to the buckle. They were my babies now. Jesus would want me to care for them.

Sunrise said, "Billy, are you sure you want to raise those wolves?" I just smiled and mounted Pal Junior. Rover seemed pleased. We all rode off together.

I forgot about the Pacific Ocean. I didn't care to see it anymore. So we decided to head east or southeast. I was ready to ride with my friends and live off the land. It was the beauty of the sky at night with stars so bright. They were so close, you could almost touch them.

We headed out of the big trees that reached the sky as I looked at a wonder of our world. It must have taken many, many years to grow trees this big. When we were miles away from the forest, I would look back and see them waving in the wind. After days of riding, stopping to kill a deer or anything that invaded our path, or sometimes a fish would get speared. Preserving what we killed would take days. We saved everything we could. The meat would have to be cooked and the skins dried. Rover would get the bones. The two wolves could eat on their own. From time to time, the rumble of buffalos could be heard. Sunrise would listen to the ground each time, then tell us which way they were going. He said don't ever get in front of a herd of the beast.

One day I think on a southeastern trail, according to the sun, Rover stopped in his tracks. His ears stood straight up and his tail straight out. Ned motioned for us to stop. He pointed in the direction that Rover was looking. Our rifles came out of the holders. We waited. No movement. Sunrise said, "Maybe it's a skunk. Stay back." I fired a shot high in the tree.

Then a frightened voice said, "Please, no shoot me," and he began to cry. He crawled out of the bush with his hands up and his head down. "No shoot, no shoot." You could tell he was afraid probably for his life.

Ned let out a whisper, "What have we got here?" Sunrise dismounted and slowly walked over to him and caught him by his ragged shirt and stood him up. He made sure he had no weapons with Rover right beside him.

Sunrise looked down and said, "It's okay, boy." Rover relaxed his posture and sat down.

The man motioned to his mouth. I think he is hungry. I got off Pal Junior and reached in the meat bag, pulled out some dried meat, and gave it to him. He grabbed it and sat down on the grass. Then we gave him some water.

Ned remarked, "Where in the world did he come from? He must have walked all the way from China." It was getting late in the day, so I suggested that we camp in this place for the night. There is grass for the horses. It sounds like I hear rushing water nearby and maybe some fish. The China man just sat and watched; I got the feeling he did not know if he was safe or not. His body would shake and tremble. His hands were crossed in his lap. I wondered what this China man had been put through. Sunrise came back with two large fish. Ned started a fire so we could cook and stay warm.

After about an hour, we gathered around the fire. We were discussing what to do about the China man. We can't leave him here. He will surely die.

I spoke up, "There must be a reason he found us or we found him. Let's get him over here and try to show that we will not harm him. Ned, would you go get him and place him around the fire?" He came over slowly and sat down. It felt like he was supposed to be with us. Why, I can't explain. All of us ate our fish, even the China man, the wolves, and of course, Rover. I was feeling very good, as we all were.

I was about half asleep when Sunrise said, "Horses are coming." We stood up and checked our weapons. Out here we did not expect anyone to be around. Two horses soon appeared down the trail. They slowed to a walk when they saw us. China man started to run. Sunrise caught him and sat him down and made a motion to stay there. His body started shaking. His hands folded in

The Last Ride

his lap, he was saying words that we could not understand. He began to cry. I laid my hand on his shoulder, which calmed him a little.

The two riders stopped and called out, "May we enter your camp?"

I whispered, "Stay ready. Yes, you may. Get off your mounts and walk toward us." This they did. I asked, "Can we help you with anything?"

"Yes, we have come for that China man. He ran off from the railroad gang. We want him back." I looked down at China man. He was still crying.

"This man is sick. He cannot travel with you now. He needs to stay with us until he gets better". The head rider gave the other rider his horse's bridle strap, then started to walk around us as if he was going to grab the China man. He was walking and not paying any attention to us. When he got to the China man, he reached for the China man. Ned poked his rifle into his stomach.

"What are you doing?" he asked. Sunrise was watching the other man standing with their two horses.

"I have come for this man and I am taking him back with me." Ned pushed the rifle harder in his stomach.

"Back off, sir."

He looked with anger at Ned and said, "You can't talk to me like that."

Ned said, "Why not?"

"I work for the railroad and have the authority to take him with me." Ned was getting angry now.

He pushed him away, saying, "This China man stays with us." Sunrise cocked his rifle. He didn't say a word. His eyes never left the man holding the horses.

Billy spoke, "Why don't you go back to your camp and just say he is gone? That way you don't have to lie to your boss."

"I am not going back without this China man," he bellowed.

"Sir, let me introduce ourselves to you two. This gentleman is Uncle Ned, and this is my brother, Sunrise. My name is Mister Bill. We are family. This China man will be another brother of mine, and no one splits the family up. You two can't do it either." Rover was just sitting and watching. The two wolves went and stood by his side, one on each side. I realized Rover is teaching them to be like him.

The China man stopped crying, looked up, and said the best he could, "My family." I knew then we would have to take him with us. I could not leave him behind.

"Just go back and tell your boss that he is gone." Billy stood up, dropped his hands by his side, and looked at the angry man. His eyes turned dark blue and he said, "Sir, are you ready to go to Satan's home? Now get on your mounts and ride. You see we are not here to kill."

The two riders mounted their horses, stared at Billy, and said, "We will not bother you again."

China man said, "Me family now."

We decided to move away from our camp site for an unwanted visitor may plan another visit. Sunrise asked Chinaman, "Can you ride a horse?"

"No, I learn." We took all the food and furs off the pack horse and placed in on the other three horses. Billy told China man that he could ride on the pack horse. It didn't take long to realize that China man could not ride. We moved slowly while China man was getting used to his mount. We were all wondering what we had done.

About two hours away from the old camp, Ned spoke up, "We need to select another site. It will be dark soon. The sun will be out of sight soon." Billy suggested that we should probably head toward some low hill that we could see behind the trees.

We were running low on food. We must find some soon. With the four of us, and the wolves and of course, Rover, it took a lot of deer and bear meat to keep us going. That problem was solved the next day. We came across a stream with beavers building a dam. We caught four, skinned them, and cooked the meat. The furs will dry in the sun in a couple of days. It will take some time to cook all the meat. China man proved to be very good at cooking, so we let him take charge of the food. The rest would see to the furs. The furs were very valuable. They would be traded for bullets and a rifle for China man when we came to a town or village.

As we rode into a small town, very few people were out that we could see or hear. The weather was cool. It had stated to snow. We stopped at a shed that had a sign half torn off the front of the building. It read, "Livery—Joe's Livery Stable."

I said, "Keep your eyes open, everyone." We pulled up inside the barn. No one seemed to be around.

Sunrise called out, "Anyone here?" Not a sound. It looked like someone had been here recently. There were stables and grass hay, a water trough, a blacksmith shop, and shoes hanging on a post. Sunrise walked toward the back of the barn with rifle in hand. His instinct seemed to tell him that someone was in the loft or maybe he could smell something. He raised his hand, and we knew what that meant. We all paid attention and cocked our guns, except for China man. He didn't know the signal. When he saw the look on our faces, he cocked his rifle.

Then Sunrise pointed toward the loft, not knowing if whatever up there was man or beast. There was a ladder in front and one in the back of the loft. Sunrise started up the rear ladder, and I started up the front ladder.

Then Sunrise called out, "Over here, Billy." I rushed over to where he was and looked down at a man and a boy in a pool of dried blood on a pile of hay straw. I checked to see if they were alive. Someone had beaten them up good.

"Let's get them down from here." After some struggle, we had them lying on an old burlap sheet. China man got some water. He washed the dry blood off their faces. We could all see that they were Indians. It looked like a father and son. They did not appear to have any broken bones, just cuts and bruises. It was getting colder. Ned found some lumps of coal in the blacksmith shop. He made a circle in the ground and put some hay straw and old dry board and placed the coal on top. He took two pieces of flint and started a fire. We gave the two some beaver meat.

It was a good place to spend some time. It had a roof over our heads, a fire to warm by, and shelter from the wind. Rover, Rock, and Grace found a bed in the hay straw. So did we. I didn't know if the man and son would be here in the morning. I could tell that they had been away from their tribe for some time. They spoke good English and understood most of what was being said. I didn't ask any questions until the next morning. I knew it could be risky to trust them, but somehow I did. I didn't think they would run away for it was too cold, besides the snow was too thick to see far. Rover, Rock, and Grace were keeping their eyes on the strangers.

The next morning in broken English, they told us their story. He, his wife, and son worked for Mr. and Mrs. Jones, Fred and Sara, for many moons. Good town—good people. All are in hiding now. Why are they hiding?

"Bad men came yesterday, robbed store, took my wife and mother, beat her, raped her, and then cut throat in front of boy's eyes. We tried to help her, but they knocked us down, beat us, and laughed."

"What do we call you?"

"My name is Wolf because I saved my chief from a wolf attacked by killing the wolf with my knife." Then he looked over at Rock and Grace. "Are they wolves?" he asked.

"These are my wolves. I raised them because they lost their mother. Rover there is training them to be like him. Do you think the bad men will come back here?"

"Yes, I heard them say we will come back tomorrow to get us another girl. I have a daughter that is hiding in the store basement now, I hope. I need to go find her."

"Let's go find her," I said.

"My boy's name is Waterfall. I just call him Fall. He went over a waterfall and is alive. Daughter's name is Bright Eyes, like her mother's."

"Everyone, stay here by the fire. Watch out for the bad men. If they show up, fire one shot. Rover, Rock, and Grace will keep watch." Rover was teaching them well. Sunrise went with me. "Ned, you watch over the boy, Fall, and China man." Sunrise and I started following Wolf Man. He went into the general store, stopped when he entered the storage room in back of the store.

He called out, "Bight Eyes, Mr. and Mrs. Jones. I am opening the door to the hiding place." Then he rolled a bag of rice over and pulled up a trap door. The first face he saw was Bright Eyes. They both began to cry. Tears flowed like water.

"Papa, where is Mama?"

"Come on out," he managed to whisper. "Mr. and Mrs. Jones, come on out." A shaking woman appeared. When she saw me and Sunrise, she screamed.

Mr. Jones grabbed her, looked up, and said, "Please don't kill us." Wolf at that time had enough composure to speak.

The Last Ride

"Okay, okay, a friend." They stared at Sunrise with fear on their faces. Sunrise just smiled and put his hand out to help them out of the hole.

Bright Eyes kept saying, "Papa, where is Mama. Where is Mama?"

I put my arm around her and said, "He will tell you in a minute."

"I want to see my mama. Please ,sir, take me to my mama." At that moment, I began to shed a tear, so did Sunrise. "Mr. Jones, would you start a fire in that potbellied stove? Everyone needs to get warm." I went outside and yelled for Fall. I think he should be with his family at a time like this. He came in a run, gave Bright Eyes a big hug as she was still crying and calling for her mama. Fall didn't say a word. He was all choked up. I yelled to Ned and China man to come on over. China man rushed over. Ned wanted to feed the horses and water them. As he started to lock the barn door, he saw three riders on top a hill and headed toward town. He pulled his pistol from his holster and fired one shot. I rushed out the door. Ned held up three fingers and pointed to the road that leads out of town.

"Stay there, Ned," I yelled. He gave me a thumbs up and moved out of sight. "Everyone, get behind the counter and stay down. You, too China man."

"No," Chinaman said, "Me, family, stand together." He picked up his rifle. I didn't say a word or say no.

As they strolled into town, I asked Mr. Jones, "Are these three the ones that robbed your store?"

He peered out the window and said, "Yes." It looked like they were headed toward the general store probably. When they got about ten yards out, I stepped out onto the sidewalk. After me came Sunrise, then China man.

The leader looked at us and said, "Well what do we have here," he said with a grin. With that the three spread out a little like they knew what they were doing.

"Gentlemen, let me introduce myself and my friends. My name is Mister Bill, and this is Sunrise, and this is Shanghai."

"Me have a new name now. Me Shanghai," said Shanghai.

"Oh, by the way, I guess you came back to pay Mr. Jones for what you took from his store?"

"We don't pay for anything. We take what we need. Only idiots like you pay for what you need."

"Sorry, sir, you will have to pay up."

"Like hell I will." By that time, Ned walked up.

"Oh, this is Uncle Ned," I said. "We are family."

"Why you look like a bunch of misfits that's acting like a no fit."

"Let me introduce myself again. My name is Mister Bill and I didn't come here to kill. But today I will if I need to. Now, gentlemen, which one of you killed Mama after raping her?" Bright Eyes screamed. Wolf came out. He walked out and pointed to the leader.

"He did it." Then Fall walked out.

"You pig," he cried. I caught his arm and held him back. They went for their guns. Two of them fell out of their saddles. The leader was all humped over about to fall off his horse. Fall went over and pulled him to the ground.

Bright Eyes came out of the store with a butcher knife crying and yelling. As she lunged toward him, Sunrise stopped her.

"It won't help, Bright Eyes," and he pulled her close to him. "Let's go inside." Shanghai handed Wolf his rifle. Wolf shot him in the head. Then he handed the gun back to Shanghai. The towns' people had been watching. Many were coming out. They must feel safe now.

Ned said, "These horses have no brand on them. I guess they are ours now. Wolf, you and Fall take the horses over to the stables, water, feed, and cur them down. We are going to need them. Maybe the town of Logan will be safer now. Wolf, tell us how you came to be in a town called Logan."

"I will after Fall and I take care of the horses, which will take an hour or so." I went back inside the general store to see if Mr. or Mrs. Jones had gained their composure. I sat down on a sack of corn and watched. Sunrise was holding Bright Eyes as she cried. He shed a tear. Then I got a toe sack and went outside to collect all the guns that the three men were carrying along with their bullets, carrying them over to the livery. I knew we would have to leave tomorrow morning and get lost in the forest.

The Last Ride

Wolf and Fall had finished feeding the horses, so we got the fire started again and sat down around it.

Wolf said, "In the morning about daylight, Fall, Bright Eyes and I will burn Mother and send her to the Spirit World."

"I will help if you like."

"No," Wolf said. "The three of us will be enough. Zuni custom. You see, many moons ago, Spaniards come to our village to look for yellow rocks. When we did not tell them where we found them, we had a fight and told them to leave. They told us they would be back with many more soldiers. In a moon or so later, they were back. We still no tell. Then they started shooting us, one at a time, until we tell.

A battle between Zuni and soldiers was on. Zuni was winner. Soldiers ran off. Many died that day. I took my wife and boy and left. Along the way here, we would stop and set up a camp, usually by a stream where fish were and deer were. Bright Eyes was born in one of those camps. One day boy was hunting and breaks his leg. I went looking for help. I went up the highest hill to look around. It was a clear day. To the east, I saw this town where we are now. The town people helped us reset leg and feed us and ask us to stay. We have been here about fifteen years. I built this livery stable. Bright Eyes and Mama would sleep in the store room and help the store owners as they were needed. I would help, too. Been a good life until yesterday. Now Mother is gone to be with the spirits. What will we do without her? I don't want to stay here anymore. This livery stable is about to fall down. It's getting pretty old."

"Why don't you, boy, and Bright Eyes come ride with us? You do not need to stay for the law might come looking for us and you. Tomorrow we must leave. You have three horses now. All look to be in good shape. I will talk to family and will let you know at dawn. If you decide to ride with us, bring Mama to the stables and then burn down the barn."

Before dawn the next morning, Sunrise, Shanghai, Ned and I were feeding and saddling our ponies to leave Logan and head east or southeast. The snow had stopped, and the sun was coming up. I was waiting for Wolf, Fall, and Bright Eyes. Then they appeared out the door of the general store. Mama was on a toe bag sheet. They were walking toward the livery.

When they got to where I was, Bright Eyes said, "We want to ride with you." Sunrise was listening. A big smile came over his face. They put Mama in a pile of hay and stripped some of the old boards off the wall of the barn. They folded her arms and covered her up.

"Saddle up," Wolf said.

"Wolf, there is a mule out back, is it yours?"

"Yes. She can be our pack mule."

It took us some time to get ready to move out. About mid-morning we were ready. Some of the towns' people had ventured out. Some brought blankets, a bonnet for Bright Eyes, and one lady gave her a scarf. They all watched as Wolf, Waterfall, and Bright Eyes thanked them. Then Wolf told them that he was going to burn down the livery stables.

"Mama is inside, and we are sending her to the big spirit." There were some gasps heard along with some tears. The three went inside to set the barn on fire. As Wolf went in, he turned and called to me, "Mister Bill, would you, Sunrise, Uncle Ned, and Shanghai come inside?"

We all circled around Mama, whose real name was Happy Face. She had become a part of the town, as I could tell by the way the town ladies were showing their love for her. Wolf asked us to join hands. He called for the Great Spirit to welcome her to be with him. Tears were flowing from all of us. Wolf chanted some words that I did not understand. Then he put some black powder on the hay straw, took two pieces of flint, and started the fire. We all went outside and watched while the barn went up in smoke. Sunrise was holding Bright Eyes, Wolf and Fall stood by her side.

There were seven of us now riding the open plains. We traveled fast the first week. I wanted as far away from Logan as I could get. But after then we slowed down. We set up a camp near a river where there was plenty of grass for the horses; fish in the river, and buffalo around. It kind of felt like home. Rover, Rock, and Grace were our care takers. If an animal came too close to our camp, they would let us know—day or night.

This camp seemed to please us all. In fact I wanted to stay there, and we did for a very long time. Until one afternoon when Ned and I were hunting on a hilltop near the camp, there were six horses down in a near valley, riding beside the river. The same river that came by our camp.

Ned said, "Looks like a war party. Probably out to steal and murder. If they came to our camp, we would have to defend ourselves." In about an hour, they were approaching. While we had a little time to prepare for their approach, first I had Bright Eyes climb a tree that the leaves would hide her. Then we hid and surrounded the camp. No one was to fire their weapons until I fired to frighten them. We had not seen any rifles on their horses, so we had an advantage, we thought. All of us were in place, except Sunrise. He wanted to talk first. He stayed in the open near the big tree just in case he had to duck behind it.

Just before they got to where they could spot our camp, Sunrise called to them. They were surprised and halted their ponies. Slowly they rode up to Sunrise. Two of the party cocked their bows. Sunrise was watching their eyes as well as their hands. He began a conversation with the leader and found out that they were Apache from farther north looking for food. The leader moved over to where we were hanging our furs to dry.

"Give us furs," he said.

Sunrise said, "No."

"Then we will take them." One of the riders pulled back his bow. Sunrise slid behind the tree where his rifle and pistols were hidden. As he did, Billy fired, and the rider fell off his horse. Then they all fell off their ponies. Slowly we inspected to see if they were all not moving. Sunrise turned his back and signaled Bright Eyes to come down from the tree. One rider lying closest to Sunrise jumped up and pulled his knife and lunged at Sunrise.

"Lookout," came a voice from the tree. As he raised his knife and was about to cut Sunrise, a rifle shot from the big tree rang out, hitting the Apache and knocking him down. When Bright Eyes reached the foot of the tree, Sunrise gave her a big hug.

Their horses had run off. Now we had the task of hiding the bodies. There could be no sign of them or our camp.

"Billy, what and how are we going to hide their bodies?"

Billy said, "Let's take them to the river rapids where the current is strongest, drop them in, and they will float way down stream. They will never be found." We loaded them on our horses and threw them in the water. Then we watched as they went down stream. "Now let's pack up and move from this camp. It is getting late," Billy said. "Let's pack tonight and head out tomorrow morning at daylight." The horses had been watered. Everyone had eaten. Rover, Rock, and Grace were anxious and ready to travel. Rock and Grace were very big now, always following Rover around. They had become a blessing to us. I felt safer with the three of them around. As usual Sunrise was helping Bright Eyes. You could tell he liked her very much.

After a few weeks, I think, we came to a town. The sign on the edge of town said Casper. We had been following a trail a week or so. There had to be a settlement on this trail. That's how we ended up in Casper. The livery barn was on the edge of the town. We rode in and met the livery stables owner. He said his name was Slay.

"How much do you charge, Mr. Slay?"

"Two bits a horse for feed and water. If you want the cured down, it will be ten cents more for each horse."

"Thirty-five cents a horse times seven," Billy said. "Two dollars, forty-five cents. Is that okay with everyone?"

"Let's do it," Ned responded. "Mr. Slay, who buys furs in Casper?"

"We have a general store in the center of town. He will buy them. Watch him though."

"Thank you, Mr. Slay I will remember your kindness. Oh, Mr. Slay, I forgot about the mule."

"I will take care of her, too, no charge."

"Thank you," said Billy. "Let's go sell our furs and then get ourselves a meal at the hotel." Casper was small, but there was a saloon, a hotel, and a general store. The same as other towns, except it lay beside a river, not by a stream.

We found the general store and all went inside, laying our pelts on the counter. The storekeeper was startled.

"Where you folks from?" he asked.

Sunrise answered, "Everywhere. We are here to sell our furs. Do you buy furs?"

"Yes," the storekeeper responded.

"Well count them and let us know what they are worth."

The Last Ride

After checking them over, he said, "Twenty dollars."

"Well," Billy said, "I guess we will take them to the next town. They are more valuable than twenty dollars."

Shanghai blurted out, "Give us honest price, or I may have to shoot up this place."

"Now, Shanghai, please be kind. I would not want you to get in trouble with the law," Ned said.

"Let me help you shoot up this place."

Billy said, "You are not going to shoot up the general store." He looked at the store owner, "Now tell me again how much you will pay for our furs?"

"I will pay five dollars a pelt."

"How many pelts do we have?"

"Twelve, sir." He turned around and looked at his friends. "What do you think?"

"Sounds about right to me," Ned replied.

"Sixty dollars cash please," Billy said. At that moment, in walked the most beautiful lady he had ever seen.

No one said a word as she went over to the store owner and said, "Hi, Papa."

"Judy, this is, would you introduce yourselves to my daughter, Judy?" Judy was not only beautiful, she also carried a pistol on her hip. Everyone gave their names, Ned, Sunrise, and Bright Eyes, who was standing close to him. Wolf, Water Fall, Shanghai. Billy couldn't speak. He just could not take his eyes off of Judy. She walked over to him, saying, "Now what is your name, sir?"

He pulled off his hat and managed to respond with, "They call me Mister Bill."

He looked into her eyes. They were dark brown. She looked into his eyes, which were sky blue. It was all quiet until Sunrise whispered, "Uh oh."

"Mister Bill," she said. "My name is Judy, Judy Wilson. My mother and father with me came here several years ago because I wanted to see more of the west land. Dad was also looking for a place to start a new business. Mother would go anywhere Papa would go. So here we are. Mama passed away last year."

"How?" Billy whispered.

"A brute pushed her off her horse while she and I were riding in the grasslands. A rider was coming toward us, so we stopped. He yelled, 'Get out of my way, you women,' and plowed his horse in between us, causing Mama to fall off her horse. She broke her back and could not make it back…That's why I wear a gun now. I hope he will show up one day. Papa has been teaching me to shoot for a long time. If he ever does show up, Papa would go after him. That is why I have to be good with a gun. I would help Papa."

"What was this man's name, if you know?"

"Lucus Rye. That is what the town people call him. He stayed here a few days after the accident. Shot up the saloon one night. A young man told him to quiet down, that they were having a poker game and we need quiet. Lucas went over and knocked his hat off. The young man told him to pick up his hat. He refused, and a right fist caught his chin and knocked him over a table. After a few moments, he staggered to his feet and yelled, 'Draw, Sonny.' The young man didn't have a chance. After that he rode out of town. Someday I will find him and I will kill him."

We left and made our way over to the hotel. The hotel sign read, "No Alcohol, Just Beer Food Anytime, Nightly Rates." I didn't want to stay there. It would cost us too much, besides we were used to sleeping on the ground. I ordered steak with a potato. So did everyone else. Even Bright Eyes. After supper all went to the livery barn where Slay was curing down the ponies and the mule. Sunrise asked if horses could stay in the stables till morning.

We turned to leave, and Slay called out, "Where are you sleeping tonight?"

Billy said, "On the ground somewhere outside."

Slay said, "You don't have to sleep out back. You are welcome to sleep on some hay. I even have a special place for the young lady." We all looked at him. It was hard to perceive that there was such a kind gentle stable keeper.

Bright Eyes said, "Thank you."

I suggested that we stay in Casper a few days and rest our ponies. They all agreed.

Ned said, "Do you want to see Judy again, Mister Bill?"

I grinned a smile and promptly said, "Thinking about it." I followed with, "This is a friendly town. Some of you can pitch in and help Slay here in the barn. You know what is to be done."

The Last Ride

"And where will you be, Billy?"

"I think I will help Mr. Wilson in the store."

"I thought so," said Shanghai with a big grin. Mr. Wilson agreed to let me work for him and made sure I didn't expect to be paid. Fine with me, I just wanted to see Judy.

Sometimes a rowdy cowboy would come in and make a fuss about the price or service. Judy and I would listen. If Papa couldn't seem to control the customers, Miss Judy and I would step out of the store room. No intention of threatening the customer or letting Papa know why we were there. All would be quiet at that time. Judy and I would have long talks. Papa knew what was going on. She finally let me kiss her, which became a daily experience. Sometimes we would go for long rides into the country. Yes, I fell in love with her. She said she loved me also.

Casper was becoming my home, but I knew it could not be. I knew that I would want Judy forever by my side. So one day in the storeroom, I asked Judy to marry me.

She said, "Yes, but Papa must approve. Let's go find out."

"Mister Bill," he said, "I know you two have fallen in love. I have eyes! Billy, are you going to stay in this town?"

"No, sir," I responded.

"Then my answer will be no."

Billy said, "I want to take Judy to be my wife and ride with me and the rest of us till we find the right spot to start our ranch. Then she will send for you when the time is right." Papa seemed sad as he looked at his daughter. Then he began to weep.

He muttered, "I knew this day would come, but I didn't want it to come." Judy started to cry.

"Mr. Wilson, I will telegraph you from every town to let you know how we are doing. Then you let Judy know how things are with you. If the town has no telegraph, I will write you a letter."

Three days later, we were standing in the little church on the outskirts of town saying our I do's. Our honeymoon was in her house. Papa had to sleep in the store. About two days had passed. There was a knock at the door.

Startled, Judy said, "Hi."

"Could we talk to you and Billy?"

"Sure." Sunrise did the talking as Bright Eyes held on to him.

"Bright Eyes and I want to be married the same as you two."

"It's about time," Billy said. "As Mr. Wilson said, I have eyes, too. Have you gotten Wolf's permission?" No answer. "Bright Eyes, we will go with you so he will know that I approve. Where is he now? In the barn? I will go get him. You stay here." A short time later, Wolf showed up with Billy. I think he knew what was on Bright Eye's mind. But she didn't speak.

Sunrise asked Wolf, "Is it okay if I marry your daughter? I want her with me always." He spoke not at all.

Then he asked, "Do you want Indian wedding or white man's wedding?" Grinning, "Of course I give you my child for you are for her."

Bright Eyes said, "Indian wedding."

The next afternoon, we all crowded into Judy's small house. Wolf had a shaker, a gourd with beans inside. The two stood together between two windows.

"Hold hands," he said. Then he held the gourd over their heads and rattled it all the way from head to toe, each one separately. He asked them to hold hands. Then he asked, "Oh, Great Spirit, these two are one now. Walk with them as one." He rattled the gourd from side to side. He asked for his knife, saying, "Give me your hands." He took his knife and drew blood in their hand. He then pressed two hands together and held it tight. "Face each other. Look into eyes, pull close to each other, hold tight. Now touch lips. Now you are married."

Judy asked, "Would you like to stay tonight in this house? Billy and I will stay in your room in the barn." It was a beautiful wedding as a tear or two were shed. Fall was quiet but no tears. His face showed sadness. He would be losing his sister. Wolf put his arm around him. "Son, just be glad she found Sunrise. Others could have been much worse. It is the Spirit's way." Rover, Rock, and Grace spent the night in the house. It seemed like they wanted to be there.

We left Casper about a week later. There were eight of us now. Eight horses, two pack mules, and of course Jesus. Mr. Wilson had given us coffee, salt, and beans. I purchased more ammunition and gave back ten dollars to cover the supplies he had given us for journey and for the bullets. Slay was going to work at the store. He turned over all the barn duties to his helper. Judy said goodbye to Papa and told him she would write or telegraph every time she could. I know it was not easy for her.

She loved her Papa, but knew it was time to say, "I'll see you Papa."

Casper was a settlement on the banks of the Platte River. We followed the river heading southeast. Judy and I were sleeping together. So was Sunrise and Bright Eyes. Shanghai and Wolf did most of the cooking. Fall and Ned liked to fish. Sunrise and I did the hunting. Judy and Bright Eyes would prepare the hides for drying. All of us would take time for target practice. It was important to stay sharp with our guns.

A lot of people traveled the Platte River, and once in a while someone would wander near our camp. No stranger could come near without Rover, Rock, and Grace warning us. As they closed in on our camp, our lookouts would meet them and let them know not to enter.

One day a couple came too close. Rock jumped on his chest and knocked him into the river's edge. Shanghai called him back to camp and gave him a bone. He picked up his rifle and walked over and pulled the man up and said he was sorry.

"You must get permission to enter our campsite."

"Was that a wolf that charged me?"

"Yes, sir, we have two of them. The other one is watching you now. Their names are Rock and Grace. They have been with us since they were born. See that dog over there? He trained them both. They are part of our family."

The lady that was with him said, "Sir, we mean you no harm. We are hungry and wanted to ask you for a bite of meat."

"Do you have any weapons on you?"

"No, my husband lost them in a poker game," she said. "I think he was cheated out of our six shooters and knives. We have nothing now, not even food, only what we are wearing and our two horses. He was going to bet the horses until I pulled him away from the table, and now we still have two horses."

"Give them some meat," Shanghai said.

Billy had been listening and walked over and asked, "Tell us about yourselves."

"Well we are from a small town called Council Bluff. My name is Marvin. My wife's name is Josey, Marvin and Josey Whittley. We just wanted to go to California. Heard everyone was rich and plenty of gold everywhere. Council Bluff was our home. Had a small ranch and were doing well until a man told me I was on his land. He said move off or die. He had six men with guns with him. I knew it was my land, but we got scared when he came back the second time and decided life was better than dying."

"Now, sir, if you will show me the man that cheated you, I want to look him over."

"He carries a big gun. Two of them do," Marvin said.

"Go point him out. I want you by my side." He strolled over to the gambler's table. "Now Marvin, tell him you want your guns and knives back."

With hands shaking and voice trembling, he said, "Mr. Gambling Man, I want my guns back and my knives, too."

"Are you crazy, man? I won them from you in a game of poker."

"Sir", Billy injected, "give him his guns and knives and all will be satisfied."

"Who are you?"

"You don't want to know."

"I am just a cowboy living off this beautiful land."

"Sir, put your hands on the top of the table. If your hand slides under the table, you are going to have three eyes." Judy had come up and stood beside Billy.

She said to the poker man's partner, "If you reach for that gun, you will have three eyes, too." Billy smiled at her. She said, "Remember we are partners, husband."

Several people had gathered around to watch with curiosity and listening to what was being said. The gambler said, "Okay, here are his guns and knives." When he laid them on the table, his hand slid under the table, and the other gentleman lowered his hands. Two shots rang out, and two men had three eyes. The crowd gasped.

One asked, "Who are you?"

"My name is Mister Bill."

"My name is Judy."

The Last Ride

"Get your guns and knives now, Marvin. You can stay in our camp tonight." Josey ran up to Marvin with tears in her eyes.

"I just knew you would be shot. Josey, we have been blessed today."

The next morning, while everyone was waking up, Marvin and Josey came out to sit with Billy. Marvin asked, "What will we do now?"

"What would you like to do?"

"I would like to be home on my ranch."

"What about you Josey?"

"I want to be with Marvin. Where he goes, I want to be there." Judy came over, gave Billy a kiss, and sat down.

Billy asked Marvin, "Do you have a deed to your land?"

"Yes," he responded. "I have it right here."

Billy took the paper and read, "The property of Marvin Whittley." Miss Judy looked it over also. Billy and Judy looked deep in each other's eyes.

Judy said, "I think we need to go to Council Bluff."

Marvin and Josey's eyes lit up. Billy said, "Let's go get your ranch back." Sunrise and Uncle Ned walked over.

"What's up?"

Judy said, "Billy and I are making a side trip to Council Bluff to get Marvin and Josey's ranch back. Marvin has a deed that says the ranch is his."

Ned said, "Sunrise and I will go, too, Billy."

"No, Sunrise, you stay with Bright Eyes. Ned, you try to keep order in the camp. I will ask Wolf to go with Judy and me." He called Wolf over. "Wolf, will you go to Council Bluff with Judy and me? We are going to reclaim Marvin's ranch. He has a paper to show that it is his."

"Yes," replied Wolf.

"Everyone, gather around, I have something to say." Billy explained the situation. Shanghai said, "Let me go with you."

"I had rather you stay here. Just Judy, Wolf and I will go to Council Bluff. Fall, take care of Rover, Rock, and Grace. Let's saddle up." Marvin and Josey were already doing just that. "Shanghai, pack us enough deer for five days. Sunrise, Ned, it will take two days to get there, one day to settle the score, and two days back. Keep going till you reach Kearney. Wait for us there, south of town."

Before long we three were ready to travel. Billy, Judy, Wolf, Marvin , Josey, and Jesus said goodbye.

I had estimated our travel time about right. We arrived at the ranch on time only to find a man and woman living there. I explained that this was not their home, that Marvin was the owner of the ranch.

The man spoke up, "But Mister Beacon said it was his and for us to live here and care of the place."

"We are going into town and tell Mister Beacon that he was wrong. When I come back by tomorrow, you best be gone."

"Where will we go?" asked the wife. "We have no other place."

Marvin spoke up, "Billy, let them stay. Josey and I will work with them. Don't throw them out with no place to go and call it home."

"Which way to town?" Wolf asked.

"That way," as he pointed north.

Wolf said, "Mister Bill, let's rest here a while, and I am hungry. Will you and your wife be kind enough to allow us to stay a while?"

"Yes," he said, "and we will get you some biscuits and honey for all of you."

It was getting late in the day, and it looked like a storm was headed our way. We went inside, ate our biscuits, and listened to Marvin and Josey tell of their ordeal with Mister Beacon. The two that were keeping house in Marvin's ranch began to open up and tell us all about Mister Beacon and the reign of terror throughout the county. He had taken over most of the homes and small ranches. His men had shot one and burned down his haystacks and ran his cattle off. Probably they were added to his herds. "No one dares to challenge his authority. His four gunmen rule the town and county. The sheriff left town, so Mister Beacon is the law. We are afraid to speak against him."

Judy and I were saddened by these tales of woe. We thanked them for the information and set out to sleep in the hay barn until morning. Marvin wanted us to sleep in his home, but Judy said we would rather sleep together in the hay loft of the barn. Judy caught my hand and told them goodnight. Wolf had watched, and I could tell he felt the sadness of the family of the ranchers that lost their homes. He had been forced from his home land.

The Last Ride

Wolf, Judy and I rode into Council Bluff about noon the next day. We went to the general store for Judy wanted to visit it. I think it gave her a warm feeling. She could almost see her Papa behind the counter. I asked the store keeper where I might find a gentleman by the name of Mister Beacon.

He said, "You don't want to mess with Mister Beacon. He is mean and has four men or gunslingers to do his dirty work."

"Where may I find him? Do you know?"

"Yes, I do. He has an office in the back of his saloon—the Beacon Saloon and Eatery." Wolf said, "Let's go find him." The saloon wasn't hard to find. There was laughter and piano music coming out into the street.

Judy said, "It sounds like there are a few drunken cowhands blowing off some steam. Give some men a few drinks and he becomes king of the world. Maybe some of them need to be brought back to reality."

"Check your weapons," Billy said. "Let's go inside."

We stepped through the door and stood for a moment and observed the happy crowd. Judy by my side and Wolf beside her. We walked over to the bar, then turned to face the patrons. A loud voice came from amid the group of men.

"We don't allow no Indians in here. So get out, Indian, now, and we don't allow no women either." We all stood very quietly.

Billy said, "Let me introduce some of my family. This is Wolf, this is Miss Judy, and I am Mister Bill. We just want to speak to Mister Beacon." Billy had already spotted him. The gentleman in the big hat and smoking a cigar. "Have any of you seen him?" All eyes turned to the man with the cigar. They all backed away from his table, except the four men. I asked the bartender, "Would you point out Mister Beacon?"

"That's him in the big hat, sir."

"Mister Beacon, I would like to know why you take the ranchers' land and cattle without paying them for their loss by threatening them with bodily harm if they do not get off of your so-called ranch? You are taking their ranch by force, Mister Beacon. Would you please give me your answer, sir?"

With a loud manly voice as he stood up, glanced right and left to check his hired gunmen, "What I do is none of your concern. Now get that Indian and that woman out of my saloon before I have you shot."

"Mister Beacon, you are a Satan man." My eyes turned dark blue, my hands fell to my side as did Judy's and Wolf's. "I did not come here to kill, but I will."

"I'll give you no answer to what I do. I answer to no one," said Mister Beacon.

"You answer to Satan, Mister Beacon." They all four went for their guns. Four shots rang out. Four gunmen fell to the floor. Mister Beacon looked around and went for his pistol. Four more shots rang out. "Mister Beacon, welcome to your home. Satan is waiting. Let's go, family. They are waiting for us in Kearney." Before Billy left, he faced the men and said, "You are free to take back your land now."

When we arrived in Kearney, we were greeted first by Rover, Rock, and Grace. The family, Sunrise, Bright Eyes, Uncle Ned, Shanghai, and Fall were all there.

Judy asked Sunrise, "Does this town have a telegraph station?"

"Yes, Miss Judy, down by the tracks."

"I would like to notify my Papa as to where we are now. Billy, I will be back after I get an answer from Papa."

"Sure, love. Shanghai, you and Fall go with her. I would be worried if she went in town alone. Fall, don't carry your gun, just your knives. They are your best weapons now. You need more practice with the pistols. Shanghai, take your pistol and rifle."

"Yes, Mister Bill, will do."

Judy sent her wire and waited for an answer. It took the longest time for her answer. Finally the telegraph agent came and handed her the telegraph.

It only read, "Daughter, come get me. Papa."

She jumped up and said, "Let's tell Bill about this telegram. It sounds urgent." While this was going on with Judy, Shanghai, and Fall, a train pulled into the station. Three passengers were exiting the train. One man looked at Judy, Shanghai, and Fall.

He said, "Lady, would you get your two boys to fetch my luggage and trunk, then take them to the hotel? Then you and I can have dinner together," he said with an arrogant tone and a wink of the eye.

Judy asked, "Where are you from, sir?"

"Why I am from Boston."

"Where is that?" Shanghai asked.

The Last Ride

"None of your business, China man!"

"My name is Shanghai, kind sir, and this lad is called Water Fall." Judy was enjoying it all.

"Come with me, young lady, I will show you a good time." Judy had had enough.

She stood up and said, "Mister, if all the men in Boston are as crude as you, the city needs some improvement in character." He pulled back his hand as if to strike her.

Fall spoke up loudly, "Sir, if you strike her, you have seen your last moon." He looked at Fall.

"What do you think you could do about it?"

"Not me, sir, Miss Judy takes care of herself." He drew back as if to strike Fall.

Shanghai punched the Boston man in the stomach and said, "Back off."

Judy spoke up, "Shanghai, Fall, we need to get to camp and show Billy this telegram. Let's go." The Boston man yelled at them and called them cowards. Judy looked at Fall and Shanghai and said, "That man will not last too long in this territory." They hurried back to camp. Judy called, "Husband, look at this wire. Papa must be in trouble." Billy looked and read.

"Let's pack up. We will head for Casper early in the morning."

Judy said, "I will go with you." Billy thought for a moment.

"Wife, my beloved, it's probably best for you to stay in camp. Papa said to come get him, and that we will do. Sunrise and I will bring him here." Judy teared up.

"But husband, I want to see Papa."

"I know you do, love. I will bring him to see you. Sunrise, will you ride with me to Casper?"

"I am ready, Billy." Then Bright Eyes shed a tear. The two ladies walked off together crying.

Billy said to Sunrise, "You think we are doing the right thing? Our loves are not taking this well." Judy and Bright Eyes walked back over to Billy and Sunrise.

This time it was Bright Eyes that said, "Husbands, we have decided that we are going with you, too." Billy started to say no. Sunrise touched his shoulder and said, "Sounds right to me." Billy looked at Sunrise in surprise and then smiled.

"If four of us are going, we will need a pack mule." Smiles were all around. "It will take us about two weeks to reach Casper."

At breakfast the next morning, Sunrise told and went over the details of the situation.

"Now Ned will be in charge of the camp while we are gone. Billy and Judy, Myself and Bright Eyes will go to Casper and bring her papa here."

It did take a little over two weeks to reach Casper. The town looked deserted. Not many people were on the street.

Billy said, "Stop! Things don't seem right in town. Let's go around and enter the town from the back. Maybe in back of the general store." Judy could hardly wait to see her papa. "Wait, love, let me check inside before you enter."

"Hurry up, dear, I will be right behind you."

"Come on," Billy said. He peeped inside but could not see anything going on.

Judy called, "Papa, Papa." Judy hurried to find Papa beaten and bruised and thin as a rail. "Oh, Papa, I am here now. You will be okay. Get some water and bread. Papa, when did you eat last?"

"Don't know. It's been a while." Bright Eyes brought the water. Papa gave her and Judy a happy smile.

Billy asked, "Where is Slay?"

"He got scared and ran off."

"Scared of who, Papa?"

"Meanest man in town. Everyone is town stays inside most of the time when he is in town. He beat Slay, cut him on his arm when he tried to help me. He comes in store when he needs bullets and never pays for anything. He takes potatoes and beans and never pays. When I ask for money, he knocks me around, also Slay." Papa looked out the window. "He must be in town now. That's his wagon in front of the saloon. He is probably on his way here after he gets drunk. Other customers have stopped shopping here, afraid he will come in store."

"Papa," as Billy was looking out the window, "do you mean the green wagon with two horses?"

The Last Ride

"Yes, he robbed the horses and wagon from Slay's livery stables. He never returned the horses or wagon. Slay asked for them back. Clyde pushed him down, saying, 'It is my horse and wagon.' He kicked Slay and walked off.

"How did you get hurt, Papa?" Judy asked.

"Clyde came to store, picked up a bag of cornmeal, started to walk out without paying me for beans." I ran to get in front of him blocking his way out the door. He hit me several times, pushed me into the counter, kicked me and laughed. Then walked out."

Sunrise asked, "Papa, what is this man's name?"

"Clyde Tucker. He has a small ranch east of town."

"Sunrise," Billy asked, "wasn't that the name of the man that tried to bushwhack us a few years ago?"

"I believe it is."

"I guess we should have hung him then."

"Well, we can do it now."

"Let's go find Slay and let him know we are in town."

Papa said, "He is hiding out in the hay loft, I think."

"Judy, you and Bright Eyes stay with Papa. Sunrise and I will go find Slay." Well it didn't take long when Billy entered the barn, he yelled, "Slay, I'm here with Sunrise. If you are here, come on down." All was quiet until some hay started falling through the cracks in the loft floor. "It's okay to come out," Billy yelled. Slay slowly climbed down the ladder and peeped through the ladder rungs to make sure it was really Billy and Sunrise.

Then he yelled, "Mister Bill, Sunrise, it's me." When he got into the light, we could see that he had a black eye, a cut on his arm, and was limping. "Never have I been so glad to see anyone as you two."

"Judy and Bright Eyes are over at the general store," explained Billy. "Where is your stable helper?"

"He left town, afraid of Clyde Tucker, I think."

"Who did this to you, Slay?"

"Clyde Tucker. Man is mean, owes me money. Will not pay."

"Sunrise and I were expecting that it was Clyde. We just wanted to make sure. Let's get you over to the store," Billy said. "Get you some water and bread."

As we all gathered inside the store, I was thankful all of us were alive.

Sunrise spoke up, "It's time for us to find Clyde." We walked slowly down to the saloon. When we arrived, I said, "Slay, you go in and ask for your wagon and team back. Papa, you go in and ask for him to pay for supplies he stole from your store. Remember, call him by name, Mr. Clyde Tucker."

"Loud and clear."

"Sunrise, you casually go in first and stand at the bar. When Clyde starts his lying, Judy and I will walk in with Bright Eyes. We want to make sure that everyone inside the saloon hears every word that is said by us to Clyde. Is everyone set? Don't be afraid. Speak with a powerful voice. Sunrise, pull your hat down over your face so he will not recognize you. Let's do it," Billy said. Sunrise casually walked in. No one paid any attention to him. He stood at the bar with his back to the crowd.

Slay walked in a little nervous but managed to say in a loud voice, "Mr. Clyde Tucker." Everything got quiet.

Clyde looked up and said, "What do you want, worm?" as he stood.

"I want my team and wagon back. You took them and never paid me for them."

"You little liar, I paid a long time ago for that wagon and horses."

Papa walks in. "Mr. Clyde Tucker, you never paid me for the bag of beans and potatoes you stole from my store." Clyde kicked his chair back.

"Why you little nobody, you are lying. I will beat you and Slay to a pulp." He started toward Papa. Slay slid to Papa's side.

"You can't whip us both." Just then Billy, Judy, and Bright Eyes walked into the saloon. Sunrise pushed his hat back. Clyde stopped in his tracks.

Billy walked over and looked Clyde in the eyes and said, "To all you gentlemen here, let me introduce my family." He pointed them out starting with Sunrise, Miss Judy, and Bright Eyes. "Some of you know Miss Judy, my wife, Mr. Wilson's daughter. My name is Mister Bill.

Now, Mr. Clyde Tucker, tell these gentlemen what Slay and Mr. Wilson said is the truth." My eyes turned dark blue and my hands fell by my side. "Are they telling the truth, Clyde?"

He was beginning to shake but answered, "They are speaking the truth."

"Mr. Wilson will take one hundred dollars for goods from his store. Slay will get his team and wagon back and twenty dollars for the rent on them. Put the money on the table now, Tucker." He counted out one hundred twenty dollars and laid it on the poker table. "Go get your money, men." All this time Judy's hands were by her side. Her eyes never left Clyde's eyes. "Okay, family, let's go now."

Judy walked over to Mr. Tucker and said, "Clyde, you are the lowlife of the town. You beat up my Papa, stole his merchandise. You are a snake in the grass. You are worthless to mankind."

Clyde said, "No woman talks to me like that." He went for his guns. Judy shot him twice. Once between the eyes and once in the heart and walked out of the saloon.

"Well done, wife." Billy walked back into the saloon and said, "Men, you can have your town back now."

Slay said he didn't want to stay in Casper for being by himself someone else might come along and beat him up again or even kill him. So he asked if he could join the family.

"Of course," I said. "Yes, if you like." He found a buyer for the stables and barn for three hundred fifty two dollars. The buyer got a good deal. Mr. Wilson also sold his store and goods for three hundred fifty dollars. Someone else also made a good buy.

We left Casper early one morning. We did not want anyone to see us leave or know which way we were headed. Mr. Wilson and Slay rode in the wagon. It took over two weeks for us to reach Kearney. We had a grand reunion when we got back to our camp. Here was Sunrise, Bright Eyes, Wolf, and Fall. Shanghai, Uncle Ned, Judy and I, and of course, Jesus. Rover, Rock and Grace had met us way down the road. They had been waiting every day, most of the day.

Slay asked, "Are these wolves our friends?"

"They think they are dogs. Rover trained them both." I said, "Rover, Rock, Grace, come here." They came over, and Billy said, "Sit down." Grace on one side laid her head in his lap. Rock, the same on his other side. Rover lay at his feet. He patted each one, and they all went to sleep, including Billy.

Uncle Ned asked Billy, "Do you think it is time to move on now?"

Billy didn't answer but told Ned, "You are in charge now. You tell us when, but if I were you, I would ask everyone." That night after supper, it was a happy time. Ned brought it up.

All of the family said, "It's up to you, Ned."

"Let's move out tomorrow," Ned replied. "Which way, south? Cold weather is coming. South will be best. We have three mules for pack animals and a wagon." We needed a water barrel and had one. It came with the wagon. Each one packed as if they were traveling alone. Saddle bags carried food, canteens for water. Some had beaver skins full of water, a feed bag for each horse and mule. Pal Junior and Pet were the leaders of the pack. I hope there will be creeks and rivers for water and fish. We would surely get some deer meat and bear meet along the way.

Kearney was left behind now. For a week or two, no one really cared about time. It all was just another day and night. From time to time, two of us would drift out into the thick brush to find something to eat. If we shot a deer, or a fox, or some other animal that was edible, we would skin it, cook the meat, and sometimes we would dry it if the sun was out. Mr. Wilson had a sack of salt he had put in the wagon. We could use it if needed to salt-down some meat. As we entered into the plains and grasslands, the trek was easy going, especially for the wagon. I felt a little vulnerable out in the open spaces. We could be seen by someone that was miles away. I asked Fall to be the head lookout. Stay ahead of us about a mile in front, but not far enough to lose sight of the rest of us. He was glad to do this. Then I asked Shanghai to follow a mile behind. Judy and Bright Eyes fanned out on each side just to make everyone feel safe. There was no fire at night or day. Smoke or fire could be seen miles away.

There was plenty of grass for the horses and mules. Water was getting a little low. We decided to ration the water—so much a day. The animals would have to be rationed also. We slowed down our pace but didn't stop. To keep going was our mantra. There were hardly any trees, only a few, not enough to hide behind. Rover, Rock, and Grace kept moving in and out of sight. They were great lookouts.

Fall came back riding hastily. "Billy, Sunrise. Big herd of buffalo off to our west." A buffalo stampede can be very dangerous. If they come our way, we had no place or no trees to get behind for protection. I had suspected as much. The Plains were great grasslands. Wolf said he could go take a look.

When he returned, he said, "Most of the herd is to our west, but there are about a hundred that would be on the east side of us. If we are quiet, let's go straight ahead and ride through them. Also, there is a river about two miles ahead. When we get to it, we can cross over. Then we should be safe in case of a stampede by the buffalo." Billy ad Judy thought hard as did all of them. Wolf advised if we are to go, we should do it now. The wind was quiet. Getting through the herd was about a half mile wide. So we did, made it through the herd of buffalo, and then I heard the crack of a rifle.

I yelled, "Get to the other side of the river, fast." The herd acted nervous, which was a bad sign. I did not know where the shot came from and I did not know in which direction the herd would run. We got to the river but couldn't cross. The water was too deep. Everyone stopped at the water's edge. The deep water was a blessing. The buffalo knew the river. They would not stampede toward the river. Then there was another crack of a rifle. That did it. The herd was on the move. Since most of the herd was to the west, they headed that way. We all got in the river's edge. About fifty buffalo got very close but none close enough to harm us. The horses and mules reacted to the noises. The wagon stayed upright. Overall we were all quiet lucky.

Ned suggested that we set up camp right here. There were trees in the water edge and some dry limbs that had fallen.

"Okay, Uncle Ned. We may stay here a day of two." Rover gave a growl, so did Rock and Grace. They all stood side by side looking down the river bank. "Everyone on guard until we see what Rover is seeing."

"Hello," came a voice. "May I come into your camp?"

"Show yourself."

"Coming in slowly," a voice said.

"Okay," Billy replied. Every gun in camp was in a hand, except Judy's and Billy's, but they knew how to get theirs in a hurry. In walked a slim man wearing a buffalo coat and pants. "Howdy, folks. I'm just out shooting a few buffalo to use their hides for something to wear and keep warm in." Judy walked up to him.

"Sir," she said, "that shot from your rifle could have gotten us all caught in a buffalo stampede, which it did. Did you not see us?"

"Yes, I saw you but figured you would make it to the river and be safe."

Shanghai walked up to him and punched him in the stomach quite hard, saying, "You could have hurt my family." Sunrise pulled him back.

Wolf said, "Be glad we were all safe, Shanghai."

"Take his rifle," Billy said, "and check him for a knife. Where is your horse and cart?" "Tied on the other side of the river. Shallow water down there."

"Let's go check it out, mister."

"What's your name, sir?"

"Silas Chilman from Texas."

"Which way is Texas, Mr. Chilman?"

"You are headed toward Texas, due south." Billy must have thought of home. He looked kind of happy, but a tear fell from his eye.

"What wrong?" Judy inquired.

Billy didn't answer for a moment and then he caught Judy's hand and said, "That is where Dad and Mama live, in the hills of north Texas."

"My husband, we must go there."

"Yes, I think I will." Judy gave him a kiss.

"I want to get to know them."

"Judy, it was about ten years ago I left my home with Uncle Ned. I wanted to go West and live under the stars, which I have done. Now home seems like a good idea. Right now I need to help Silas Chilman collect the two downed buffalo. We can use the meat and some of the hides. Ned, you and Wolf, Judy and Bright Eyes, keep guard at the camp site. The rest of you come with me." The next two weeks we were all quite busy, but we did find some time to fish. It was a happy time for us. A chill in the air was telling us to move on South. Silas asked if he could join our family and go as far as Garden City.

"What do you think, Sunrise? Should we trust him?" Ned said, "It will be better for him to be close by than for him to follow with that big rifle." His rifle had furnished us all with a lot of buffalo meat.

As it turned out, all of us agreed that he could join us. Besides, he knew the way to Garden City. I did not let him keep his rifle. I put him and his cart

The Last Ride

on point but kept Fall in front of him. We kept the same regiment as always. Judy and Bright Eyes on the sides, Shanghai in the rear, Wolf will be keeping an eye on Silas. The weather moved in the third day we were out. The rain was cold. Our fur coats were keeping us warm enough most of the time. We soon entered into a heavily thick wooded area. I called the look out back in. I did not want them out of my sight; keep a lookout but close in.

Silas took a slight right turn, which was not due south. "Wolf, do you see what Silas is doing?"

"Yes," he said. "He is turning west or southwest." We went on a hundred yards or so.

I said, "Stop. Something is wrong. Everyone, spread out and hide behind a big tree." Silas whipped his horse and ran out of sight. Then I heard horses coming toward us. It sounded like several. "Wolf, how many do you think?"

"Sounds like may be six."

"Silas had led us into a trap. Papa, you and Slay lie down in the wagon. Hold on to the reins. Try to keep control of the wagon. Here they come." Then I glanced to my left and saw two more slipping in from the other side. I yelled, "Judy, Bright Eyes, Shanghai!" I pointed toward the riders. Judy put her hand and fingers and pointed to her eyes. I knew then she had spotted them. They were expecting us to be around the wagon trying to protect our cargo. They stopped in surprise.

I yelled, "Hands up!"

They shot at my voice. We opened fire, and eight bandits fell off their mounts. Thinking we were dead, Silas came riding up. When he saw the situation, he turned to run but not far. Shanghai stepped out and fired. Silas fell out of his cart. His hose kept running.

"All right, let's get back to the main trail. Unsaddle the ponies and run them off. We want to get on down the trail as fast as we can." Fall found the right trail, and we moved out. I wondered how many others had fallen prey to those bandits. They acted so confident. I think they had robbed before but will not ever again. They are with their leader. Satan has won.

"Judy, my love, how many are there of you?"

She said, "Our family is eight strong."

"No, nine, my wife, Jesus is riding with us." As we spoke, Judy gave him a hug. Garden City can't be too far ahead.

We did reach Garden City about a week later. Since we knew then that we were going in the right direction, I recommended that we not go into the town. Sunrise agreed, and all said they agree. My reason was if no one sees us, we could not be connected to what happened in the forest. We kept going until we reached the far side of the river.

"Let's set up for a couple of days and stay out of sight. Here we can fish and hunt and rest as needed."

The next day, two men in a canoe were drifting down stream. One of them spotted our fire.

They yelled, "Hello." They pulled into the bank. "Haven't seen anyone in a week. Do you mind if we visit a spell?"

"Where have you been?" Judy asked.

"Been out west. The last town we were in was called Pueblo on this same river."

"Are you hungry?" Shanghai asked.

"We could stand a little food," one said. "I will give you a pelt."

Billy answered, "No charge for food. Tell us who you are and where you hail from." "Lots of places. Don't remember them all. Our home where Pa and Ma live now is in Tennessee. This is my brother, Aaron, and I am called Joseph. I am the oldest. Ma read the bible every day. She liked the name of Joseph and Aaron. We have another brother, but he was kinda wild. He left home one day mad at the world. Never was satisfied with anything. Never listened to anyone, and if he did, they were always wrong. Ma said he must be touched in the head." "What was his name?" Judy asked.

"We two are part of the Rye Clan. His name was Lucus, Lucus Rye. Have you ever heard of him?"

Judy heard the name and stood up and asked, "Where is he now?" Her hands were shaking.

"What is your name?"

"Judy Wilson."

The Last Ride

"Judy Wilson, my brother is gone now. He got drunk one night in the town of Laramie, was killed in a gun fight. He always thought he was the best. But he wasn't." Judy stepped back, thinking they must never know about Mama and Lucus. He paid the price, I guess, he was a little touched in the head.

Rover, Rock, and Grace never took their eyes off the two strangers and watched as they got into their canoe and floated down stream. They waved to us as they left.

Ned said, "I suggest that we leave this campsite tomorrow. Someone from Garden City will spot us. We don't need that." We left the next morning heading south. I was hoping I would soon be in Texas. All of a sudden, I was homesick. I wanted to see Dad and Mama. I felt I was being led back home. Our lookouts were placed, front was Fall, back was Shanghai, on each side was Judy and Bright Eyes. Do not get out of sight of the family.

For some time all was good, no bandits, no travelers just peaceful and lovely land until about midafternoon. We heard a squeal of what sounded like a lady screaming.

Wolf said, "Someone is in trouble. Should we go find out, Billy?"

"Yes."

Sunrise said. "Which way?"

"Sound came from over there."

"Sound came from over there." Then we heard it again.

The three of them headed in the direction of the scream. Then we saw her and two white men. They were cutting her clothes off. We rode in fast. They stopped cutting her clothes and just stood there. They were really surprised to see cowboys in this area of this wilderness.

The one that was holding the knife said, "This is none of your business. Go on your way, strangers."

"It is now!" Wolf said. He threw the knife at Billy. Billy ducked. Then he went for his gun. Billy's eyes turned dark blue, his hands fell by his side.

He said, "I see you are a Satan man," and shot him between the eyes. "May the devil welcome you home."

Wolf was holding the other man in check. Sunrise was helping the lady up and covering her body with her clothes the best he could. She was hysterical. Billy walked over to see if the horse had a brand on it.

Finding none, said, "Sunrise, would you take her to our wagon and see to her wounds? Take this horse, it's hers now."

The lady said "My husband, my husband."

"Where is your husband?"

"They tied him to a tree and left him for the wolves."

"Which way?"

"I am not sure."

"Wolf, bring that man over here." Billy looked at him and said, "You are going to show me the tree that you tied her husband to."

"I don't know."

"You better know, or you will join your partner in hell."

Billy had the knife he had thrown at him. He walked closer and said, "What is your name, Sonny Boy? Why are you here with the man lying on the ground?"

"I don't really know him, I just met him a couple of days ago. He said, 'Let's ride to the west to the open spaces.' I didn't know he was that kind of person."

Billy said, "Take us to the tree now. Get on your horse and lead out. If you try to run, you will never make it. If you want to live, take me to the tree you tied her husband to." Wolf and I rode on each side of his horse.

At first he began to say, "I can't find the spot." Billy leaned over and smacked him on the side of his head.

"Think, Sonny."

Then I heard a voice, "Help, help." There he was, afraid and helpless. When he saw Sonny Boy, he began, "No, not you."

I dismounted and walked over and said, "We are here to help you." His eyes began to fill with water and tears fell. He looked at Sonny and cried, "That man, that man."

"We know," I said.

Then I looked at Sonny and asked him to get off his horse. He panicked and punched his horse Wolf caught the bridle, reached back, and knocked him off his horse.

The Last Ride

Billy asked the frightened man, "What is your name, sir?"

"I am Biscuit."

"Your wife is safe, Biscuit. We will take you to her. Where are your horses?"

"They ran off, or the other man ran them off."

"Well, this horse has no brand or owner, so he is yours now. Let's go back to family, you, too, Sonny." When Biscuit saw his wife, they collapsed into each other's arms. They couldn't stop kissing and crying. "Fall, would you watch this bad man?"

"Sit down," Fall said. The bad man was shaking and frightened.

"Rover, come here." I pointed to the bad man and said, "Watch him." Rock and Grace were there, too. They went and sat down around the stranger.

"Are these your wolves?"

"What does it look like?" He didn't answer. Bright Eyes and Judy were now talking with the crying lady. I thought to myself, *Two of the best*. Helping a new friend. Judy asked her name. "Cleo," she whispered.

"I am Judy, and this is Bright Eyes, and the rest that you see is our family. There is one riding with us you can't see, and that's Jesus and His angels."

"Could we join your family?"

"That will be up to the family to decide, Cleo. Where do you two hail from?"

"New York City."

"How did you find your way here?"

"First we headed South from New York. Got down to Virginia, then realized that most of the land was owned by big time plantation men, a class of people that looked down on almost everyone. Biscuit said there has to be a better place to live. We headed west, hunted, fished, and trapped our way here. We've been living off the land so to speak for over two years best I can figure."

Sonny all of a sudden jumped up and started to run. "No!" Billy called out. He could not make it for Rover, Rock, and Grace would not let him get away. He headed toward a swampy area. "No!" Wolf cried out. "Snakes." He jumped in the muddy water right in a bed of water moccasins. They were all over him in a split second. He didn't have a chance. At least a dozen bit him. He crawled out of the water and lay on the bank. He started shaking and then went into shock.

The last words he spoke were, "Tell Ma I'm sorry." Those words hit us all hard, even Cleo and Biscuit. A young man's life lost. I wonder why and where he was going, none of us knew. It could be down or up. Everyone was solemn at supper, not much talk. Biscuit and Cleo also were solemn. It was almost like they longed to be with the family.

We decided to stay in this spot another day or so. I think it was to see how Cleo and Biscuit fit in with all of us.

I called Judy aside the first night and asked, "Do you think we should ask Biscuit and Cleo to ride with us?"

She thought and said, "It is fine with me. We will ask the rest of the family at breakfast."

Early in the morning, I asked Biscuit and Cleo if they would like to join our family and ride with us. Judy and I knew we were headed home. I had big plans for us all but kept them to myself. They asked me where we were headed.

I said, "South." I think they knew that was Texas.

"Yes," they both said at once. At breakfast the family will have the final say, so I will ask them. A little later, when all were awake, I asked them.

"Family, Biscuit and Cleo would like to ride with us as we travel south into Texas." All was quiet. Then Bright Eyes smiled and raised her hand. Before anything else was said, Ned walked over to them.

"Biscuit, Cleo, if we vote to include you two in the family, I have to ask you something. We will demand your love and loyalty and stand by the family at all times."

"Ned, your family saved our lives. We are already loyal."

"You two probably know us all by now, but this is who we are."

"I am Billy, better known as Mister Bill. This is Judy Wilson, my lovely wife. This is Sunrise and his lovely wife, Bright Eyes. This is Uncle Ned; he is from a Georgia plantation. This is Shanghai. He is from China. This is Wolf, originally from the Zuni tribe, and his son Water Fall. Next is Mr. Wilson, Judy's father. This is Slay from Casper. Ten of us will be twelve if you two come along."

"I vote them in," Ned said and then there were yesses all around.

"Thank you, thank you," came from Biscuit and Cleo.

The Last Ride

"You are in," Billy said. "Now let me quote you our loyalty pledge. You will at no time turn against the family and stand by each other through thick and thin or come what may. You will learn how to shoot, both pistol and rifle. Do you understand?"

"Yes," replied Biscuit and Cleo.

"Sit down here, you two. Rover, Rock, and Grace come here. You three will now protect Biscuit and Cleo for they have become part of our family." Billy pointed to himself and then took their hands into his and said, "Family now. You two lay your hands on them, and now you are their friends. Call them by name—Rover, Rock, and Grace."

For some time we continued our way south. The trails were easy to follow now. Many a horse and buggy had been up and down this road. All the grass was gone.

"A sign on the side of the road, " yelled Shanghai. I rushed up to see what it said. There was only one word – Oklahoma.

"Judy, come look. We are almost home." A few miles ahead was a river that Billy knew. He always called it the North River. "Everyone, we will be home in a week or two. Let's camp here by the river for a couple of days. I will be happy to stop and rest for a while." Just about all jumped in the river. It had been a while since we were able to bathe. Judy and I went around the bend for time alone and a bath. Sunrise and Bright Eyes went farther. Soon we were all spread out for a half mile along the river bank.

Biscuit and Cleo started a fire. Wolf and Fall came back with fish. It was a celebration, but we were not there yet. I was hoping it would not be long.

Wolf said, "We will need to find a shallow spot in the river so we can get to the other side."

"We will look tomorrow," Shanghai, smiled. Everyone agreed, tomorrow. "Rover, Rock, Grace, check out the area."

As he spoke, Billy turned all the way around with his arm and hand pointing out. "Go," he said. Then all three leaped forward. "Slay, keep an eye on them if you can. Call them back in about fifteen minutes."

It was hard for me to sleep. Soon I will get to see my mama and papa. I don't know how long I had been away from home to see the west, which I have. I got up and went over to Ned. He couldn't sleep either.

"Uncle Ned, when we left, I didn't know if we would make it home again. Really didn't care at that time."

"We have had some adventure, Billy. We rode through the west and back."

We were planning to stay at this camp about three days. But I grew restless thinking about my home. I asked the family the next morning if it would be okay with them if we packed up and start down the road again. All of us were gathered around the breakfast fire eating cold deer meat.

Fall being younger said, "I'm ready."

"Yes, Billy, I think we are all ready and rested." It took most of that morning to pack all the food, getting water, feeding the horses and mules, and much more. There were twelve of us now. It's kinda hard for me to understand how we went from two, me and Uncle Ned, to a family of twelve. Slay and Biscuit were busy looking for a shallow spot in the river. There had to be a sand bar somewhere nearby. Biscuit came back a short time later with no news of a shallow spot. "Billy," he said, "just down where the river has a long straight stretch I think we might cross there."

"Sunrise, if you will, check it out with Biscuit and see if it will be safe." When they returned, the answer was yes, it is a good spot.

It was about noon by the time we were on the other side of North River. All of us knew what to do while we were traveling: Fall in front, Shanghai in back, Judy and Bright Eyes on the sides, Rover, Rock, and Grace all over the place. I knew where we were most of the time, but so much had changed while I was away. The hills and valleys didn't look the same.

We were in Texas now, and soon we would be at the A.S.B. Ranch, home. Fall came rushing back.

"Billy, some cowboy up ahead, also about a dozen head of cattle."

"Stop everyone and try to be quiet." The three of us slowly got to a place where the cowboys were and the cattle observed. Just two cowboys and the cattle were there. I wonder why they were here in a thick forest with no grazing land for the cows. "Let's let them pass on. Check to see if they are branded." Fall slid off his pony and got closer, so he could see the brand on the cows. He came back in a few minutes.

"Mister Bill, they are branded, but they do not all have the same brand."

The two cowboys and the cattle went down the hill. Where from there I could not tell.

"Let's go back and keep going south. My home is near Pampa, Texas, about 100 miles from here. To get back to the family."

Ned called out, "All is well, let's go." One hundred miles. About four days or so until we reach home. We still had another river to cross, if I remembered correctly.

I rode over to Judy, "My love, one more week." She knew what he meant.

It was just that. In less than a week we rode up to a sign that read, "A.S.B. Ranch." It looked a little crooked with bullet holes in it. I guess someone had used it for target practice.

"Everyone, gather around. This will be your new home. It's only a few miles to my house."

Judy said, "Husband, a new start in all our lives will be here on this land."

Billy said, "We are going to have the biggest and best ranch in Texas. Mount up, let's go home." Soon I could see the house. He slowed his horse to a walk and stopped. No one was in sight. "Nathan," he called out. No answer. "Nathan," he called out again. All was quiet.

Then someone called out, "What do you want?"

"Nathan, is that you?"

"Who wants to know?"

"It's me, Nathan, Billy."

"I don't know but one Billy, and he left home ten years ago."

"Well he is back now."

"Get out where I can see you well." Billy stepped closer to the barn and stopped. Then three cowboys came out of the barn door. Nathan was in front. He stared at Billy. "Is it really you?"

"Yes, I've come home."

"I thought I would never see you again. Are you here to stay, Billy?"

"Yes, I am here to stay." They gave each other a handshake and a hug. Ned walked up. Nathan's eyes grew even larger.

"Uncle Ned!" They shook hands and hugged.

"Where are Dad and Mama?" Billy asked. About that time, he heard his mama's voice. She had been watching through the kitchen window. She burst out of the kitchen door.

"Billy, my son."

"Yes, Mama, I am back." She was crying, and so was Mister Bill.

"Son, son, I have missed you so." She called out, "David, David, Billy is home." Out walked his dad. He had a homemade stick to help him walk.

He started crying, "Billy, it is you?"

"Yes, Dad, I am home." The three of them were holding on to each other for the longest time. Then Ned walked over, and Mama burst out crying again and so did Dad.

"Uncle Ned, you are home, too."

"Judy, would you please come meet my mom and papa? Dad and Mom, this is Judy, my wife."

"Oh my, Billy, she is so beautiful." Then there were hugs all around.

Billy called to Nathan, "Come over and meet Judy. Judy, Nathan is one of my oldest friends. This is my wife, Nathan. All of these people you see here are my family and friends. By the way, what is the name of the cowboys? I never knew their name. Are they the same two that were here when I left?"

"Yes, Billy, they stayed. They found a home here."

Nathan called out, "Webb, Del, come here. You remember Billy?"

"Yes," Webb said. "Good to have you back, Mister Bill."

"I want you to meet everyone with me. First is Sunrise and Bright Eyes, they are married; next the man from China, Shanghai, next is Wolf, the man that fought a wolf, his son, Water Fall. Next a married couple, Biscuit and Cleo, and Mr. Wilson, Judy's father, then Slay, Mr. Wilson's partner. Most of all these three – Rover, Rock, and Grace, our guardians at all times."

"I know Raven, but these two are wolves."

"Yes, they are." Billy called them over, reached down, and rubbed their heads and back. "Don't be afraid." Dad and Mama did just that. Nathan got on his knees, and they came up to him. Webb and Del patted their heads.

Nathan put all the horses in the east pasture. Everyone will sleep in the barn tonight. Webb and Del killed a calf for a home coming.

The Last Ride

"Where is Pal, Nathan?"

"She is in the east pasture. I will put Pal Junior in the pasture first. I know he wants to see his mother." Pet was next to go free in the pasture. All the horses followed. I couldn't believe I was back home after ten years.

After supper Billy called Nathan, Webb, and Del and Dad over to inquire about the condition of the ranch. Billy didn't see many cows around.

"What happened?"

"Son, someone is stealing a few of our cows each week."

"How many have you lost, Dad?"

"Near as I can tell, about twenty-five."

"Do you know who took them?"

"No, but they tell me a man in Amarillo, who is a big cattle buyer and seller, has been buying a lot of land around here. When all of a rancher's cows are gone, they sell their land and leave."

"Have you lost any bulls?"

"Yes, two. I only have one left. I had over a hundred cows and three bulls. Now it's down to seventy-five and one bull."

"What do you think, Nathan?"

"I believe someone steals the cows and bulls, so the rancher cannot multiply their head with new calves."

Billy said, "Sounds about right to me. Webb and Del, get everyone together. I have something to go over with the family." They went out and told everyone that Billy would like to hold a family meeting, including his dad and mama.

"Nathan, would you tell Mama to bring that blue bolt of fabric that I saw in the kitchen?" It took about a half hour to get the family together by the barn. "Before we start celebrating tonight, there is something that must be done first. Everyone is a family member and has heard our pledge of loyalty, except Nathan, Webb, and Del. Sunrise, would you repeat our pledge for these three?"

"Sure, Billy. You will at no time turn against the family and stand by each other through thick and thin or come what way. You will learn how to shoot, both pistol and rifle. Do you understand?"

"Yes," they all said.

Next Billy said, "Mama, bring me that bolt of blue cloth so everyone will know that you are a family member. Everyone will wear around their necks this blue cloth, so everyone will know that you are a family member. Mama, would you cut a twelve-inch piece for us all? We will need fifteen strips now. Tie it around your necks please." All were soon wearing a blue bandana. "Together we can be a force as long as we stand together. Let's start building your cabins. Winter is coming. Let's get started soon. Build your cabins in a line next to the tree line. Let's build a bunkhouse next to the barn on the right side next to the east pasture and enlarge the barn for more stables. Nathan will help you with your plans. He also knows where the straight trees are. We can make this the largest ranch in Texas. Tomorrow we will get Dad's cattle back. Shanghai, are we ready to eat?"

"Yes, Mister Bill."

The next morning, Nathan, Ned and Billy set out set out to find the lost cattle. Billy was going to where he had seen all the cattle with different brands and follows the trail to where they were. They found the herd in a canyon that had been fenced off. There must have been a hundred heads within the fence. There were three cowboys camped out of the side of a hill.

"Let's go pay the three wranglers a visit."

"Wait," Billy hesitated. Two riders were approaching the camp from below the herd.

As they came closer, Nathan said, "The rider in the big hat is the cattle buyer from Amarillo. His men are stealing cattle, then he probably is selling them in the Amarillo stockyard."

"Let's watch for a while." Then Billy said, "Lets ride in slowly like we are just passing by." They saw us riding up and laid their hands on their guns.

The buyer asked, "What are you doing here?"

Billy said, "We are here to get our cattle back. I see some that have my brand on them. Don't go for your guns if you want to live." "These are my cattle – you can't take any of them." "Well," Billy said, "Dad lost twenty-five to rustlers, so we want those twenty-five and twenty-five more, plus two bulls.

The Last Ride

Now, you two cowboys, take your gun belts off and cut us out fifty head and you will help us take them home to Dad's ranch."

"You can't do that," the buyer yelled. Then he and the wranglers went for their guns. Billy shot them both between the eyes.

"Gather up their weapons and check to see if their horses are branded. If not let's take them home to our ranch. Once we get our cattle on the way home, let's tear down the wire fence and let the rest of the herd find their way home." It took us all day and into the night to reach the A.S.B. Ranch.

We herded all the cows into the east pasture, which now was about 1,000 acres. Soon we would need more acres as our herd grew larger. There was lots of work that had to be done on the A.S.B. land.

The two wranglers that helped bring the cattle home came to Billy and asked, "Could we work for you?"

"Why? "Billy asked.

"We have nowhere to be, and here we may find a home. Before we did not know that Mr. Long was dirty. It was just a job to us."

"What are your names?"

"Frank and Ben." Billy thought a while and then called Sunrise.

"Would you tell these two that in order to be one of the family, they have to take the pledge?" Sunrise told them to stand before him and listen.

"You two are not just joining us to be part of our family, but this you must do. You will pledge your loyalty to us all. You will at no time turn against the family and stand by each other through thick and thin or come what may. You will learn how to shoot both pistol and rifle. Do you understand?"

"Yes."

"Then give Mister Bill your hand. Go ask Mama to give you a blue cloth and wear it at all times, so everyone will know you work for Mister Bill and family."

This was the beginning of what was to become the largest ranch in Texas. Everyone had a job. Sunrise, Ned, Shanghai, Wolf, Biscuit, and Fall each had a special responsibility. Mr. Wilson and Slay were purchasing agents. Bright Eyes and Cleo supervised the food preparation, along with Webb, Del, Frank, and Ben. Everyone wore blue bandanas; Mama kept blue cloth around, and we never ran out.

One day the local sheriff came to visit. I did not go outside to visit with him. I let Ned visit with him and his two deputies. He wanted to take a look at the cattle. Ned explained to them that they were on A.S.B. Ranch land and we could not let them.

He said, "I am going to look at the herd."

Sunrise and Wolf came out and stood by Ned. The rest came out and stood around.

Judy came out and said to the sheriff, "Sheriff, you are on our ranch land. You may leave now if you wish, and if you want to visit again, you will need to get permission from Mister Bill. We believe in law and order and will do no wrong. You don't need to be on this ranch. We will take care of us all."

Billy came out the door and said, "Sheriff, I see you have met my wife, Judy. I would think about what she said. By the way, they call me Mister Bill." The sheriff looked around. "Mister Bill, I will not bother you again."

The word got out that the A.S.B. Ranch was a safe place to work and live. Rover and Rock were around, but Grace was nowhere to be found. Bill became alarmed. He called Grace several times. Finally he said "Rover, Rock, find Grace. Find Grace." They headed toward the barn and west around back and stood over a stack of old logs. They are just logs. Maybe a fox or something was hiding beneath. When he got closer, he heard a whimper. He got on his knees and looked under the logs and he thought, *Grace, when and how did this happen?*

"Judy, Judy, come see." She heard and came in a rush. Then she stopped in her tracks. "Look what Grace has given us—four more wolves. We need to bring some food for Grace. Better yet let's take them into the kitchen for safety. Rover and Rock need to be with her, they are family." Billy thought about the time he first saw Rock and Grace and the love he had for them. Now he had four more to love.

Almost every day Billy and Judy would mount Pal and Pal Junior and ride together inspecting fences and buildings, and when they could, they would go down by the pond and sit and hold each other. It was their time to be alone. They loved each other with all their hearts.

The Last Ride

One day a stranger rode quietly on the ranch land and came close to the home of Dad and Mama. A bell rang. We had set up a warning system. Everyone would be on alert.

Nathan walked out and said, "May I help you?"

"Yes," he said. "We have come to take your cattle."

Nathan calmly asked, "How do you expect to do that?"

"Me and six comrades here will just take them."

"Did everyone hear what he said?"

"Are you ready?"

"Yes." All must die today or they will be back. Billy and Judy walked out.

"Sir, what did you say?"

"I am going to take your cattle."

"Please try, sir, if you'd like." He was holding his hat over his gun hand. When his elbow moved, Billy shot him off his horse. He hit him between the eyes. Then several rifles fired, and six more rustlers lay on the ground. "Check the horses for brands. Get their weapons and take their bodies and throw them in the pond." The horses had no brand on them, so they became ours. "Nathan, heat up the branding iron and put our mark on them."

Biscuit called out, "Billy, one of these bandits is still alive. He looks like a kid, no more than fourteen or maybe some older."

"Don't shoot him," as he lay on the ground. Billy thought there has to be a reason for him being alive. "Bring him to the barn, Biscuit. Cleo, would you and Slay see to his wounds? If he survives, I will ask him some questions. His answers could help us protect ourselves and the ranch. He is a long way from home."

Slay came over and told Billy and Judy, "The bullet went through his left shoulder just above his heart. He may survive."

"Slay, will you and Papa take care of him for us? Watch him."

Slay and Papa said "Of course, daughter."

A week later, the kid from Mexico was talking, and it looks like he will make it. Most everyone seemed pleased and glad he didn't die. It was time for us to know how he became a cattle thief. Ned wanted to ask if he might be the one to ask where he was from and how did he get involved with the gang of thieves. He was too young to be a bandit. Ned has such a kind heart.

"My name is Rio Cruz. My home was Monterey, Mexico. My family was poor, and we had no food, so my brother Carlos and myself left home to come to Texas. We just wanted to work and set up a home again. We crossed the Rio Grande and kept going. We stole a cow or two along the way. Papa said it was wrong. It was necessary if we were to live. We made it to a small city called Lubbock in hopes we could work and make it our home. They did not like Mexicans. They ran us out of town, yelling, go home. Get out of our town.

Taking shots at us, so we ran" Everywhere we went, the towns' people would chase us away. Finally when we got to the Red River, we stopped and hid along its banks. Fishing was good, so we stayed there for a long time until we were spotted. Cowboys came and chased us again.

Later we saw some cowboys from Mexico, and we thought we would ride with them. Two days later, I heard the head honcho telling the others about a ranch that had a lot of cows, so they said, "Let's go get them and sell all of them." Fear came over us.

Dad says to Mother "We are not in good company."

"We sneaked out to our horses and rode off fast. In a short distance, I stopped, telling them to ride on. I would delay the other men and give them enough time to get away. The head honcho was not mad. I told him that Mom and Dad just wanted to go home. Let them go. They are too old to help us rustle cattle anyway. I joined up with them in hopes of making a few pesos. That was wrong, but then they would not let me leave. I don't know where my family is. I should have kept on riding with them."

"You are here now," said Judy. "Rest and get well."

"Thank you." Judy left and called Ned.

"Ned, keep an eye on him until until we are sure of him."

"What is your name, Lucky?" Ned asked.

"Pedro."

The Last Ride

Billy came over and told him, "As soon as you are able, you will be needed to help in the stables. If we are going to feed you, you will be expected to help out where you are needed." Billy noticed he showed a slight smile.

"I will be glad to."

"You can call me Mister Bill for now. Rover, Rock, and Grace will be watching you all the time, so make friends with them. Put your hands on each of them."

The four new wolves were growing fast and being taught by Rover, Rock, and Grace. Mostly they were kept in the kitchen for safe keeping. Billy, Judy, and others played with them so much of the time so that they would not be afraid of us. We gave the four names as soon we could tell them apart—Hero, Spud, Alert, Sammie. They are all loved.

Two weeks later, Rover, Rock, and Grace stuck out across the east pasture. They spread out and stopped. Two riders were approaching across the pasture. Sunrise and Wolf were already on their way to find out who was visiting the ranch. The two strangers stopped and raised their hands. Sunrise observed the surroundings to make sure there was no one else there. The man spoke. "My name is Jose, and this is my wife, Marie. We are looking for our son."

Shanghai slid off his pony, took the man's rifle from the holder, and pointed it at him, saying, "Give me your other weapons."

"Here is my knife."

"What about her?"

"Give him your knife, Marie."

"Are you hungry?" Ned asked.

"Yes," was the reply.

"Come with us then."

When they got to the barn, a loud voice called out, "Papa, Mama, I am here." Jose and Marie slid off their horses. Marie called out, "My son, my son." Tears fell as they hugged and cried. Ned did not like to see anyone's want for food. I think he was remembering his days as a slave. As he watched the three and their joy, he stepped aside and shed his own tears. Billy noticed and went to his side.

"My friend, we are your family now." He touched his shoulder and smiled. The loyalty of all that wore the blue bandanas was beyond belief.

After Jose and Marie had eaten, Billy asked to hear their story. Marie started.

"Jose and I and Pedro left Monterey about a year ago in search of a safe home. Our village had been overrun with Mexicans murdering, stealing, burning our homes. Jose, Pedro and I fled in the middle of the night and made it to the Rio Grande Rover and into Texas. Our hopes were high, our new safe life, we would find in Texas. Place after place would run us out of their town, so we kept moving hoping to find a place to stop. Even our fellow countrymen did not like us. If it had not been for Pedro we would not be alive today." All this time Marie was crying.

"One night, when we were camping with some of our Mexican friends, I thought I heard Poncha laying out plans to steal your cattle. He said there is a ranch with the brand A.S.B. We will go and take their cows and sell them. Everyone was listening to his story.

"How did you find our ranch?"

"Marie and I were camping near the bank of a river that we had just crossed, hid out in the thick brush where we could fish and rest. Sometimes we had to hide as some riders and canoes came down in the river. One afternoon two men stopped near our camp to let the horses water. They were talking about where they were headed now. One, a red bearded, long haired, looked mean, said "Do we really want to go to Amarillo... into Oklahoma?" 'Pampa,' the other explained. 'That is where the A.S.B. Ranch is located. Everyone that lives or works there wears blue bandanas. Everyone around knows about the blue bandanas. You don't mess with a blue bandana. The ranch is run by a man called Mister Bill and some very loyal partners. They call themselves a family. You want to go and get a job as a ranch hand there. It could be a good life and maybe find us a wife and settle down and have kids. I don't know if I am ready to settle down yet. Let's try Amarillo first. If you like." Then they rode off. Marie and I looked at each other.

"Those two just told us where to find the ranch we are looking for–the A.B.S. Ranch. Our hope was that we could work on this ranch and find a home." Judy walked over and stood by her husband.

"What do you think, Mr. Billy?"

He pulled her close and said, "I'll leave it up to you, sugar plum." Billy called Nathan over. "Nathan, you are the foreman, so you should have the last say about anyone we add to the family. Look them over carefully for a decision will have to be made soon. Make it after it is discussed with the family." Nathan went over to Jose and Marie. "Bright Eyes and Cleo, would you take Marie and let her help in the food preparation in the kitchen?" By now we were cooking mostly outside near the hay barn. "Fall, you and Biscuit take Jose and check on the fences. You three ride together, but be back before sundown." Nathan would not send anyone out alone.

Mr. Wilson and Slay went over to Nathan and asked, "What do you want us to do, Mr. Foreman?"

"Mr. Wilson, you are special, you are Judy's father; and Slay, here is your best friend. Go into town tomorrow and buy the supplies we need, especially a bolt of blue cloth. I think we are going to need more blue."

Billy noticed that Judy had been in good spirits lately and was smiling a lot. They sat down to supper in the kitchen as usual playing with Hero, Spud, Alert, and Sammie with Rover, Rock, and Grace under the table, David and Ruth were each holding a wolf, which had become a nightly ritual.

"Honestly, honey, my dear love, why are you so happy these days?" Ruth knows already. He looked at his Mama. "Mama knows what?"

"She will have to tell you, son."

"Tell me what, my love?" Judy spoke.

"Billy, my one and only, I am pregnant." She touched his face as she said those words. Billy stood up and held her tight. Then kissed her.

"That is the best news I think I have ever heard," Billy said with tears in his eyes.

"Good news all around," Dad remarked. "I am going to be a granddaddy."

"And I am going to be a grandma," Mama said with excitement in her voice.

All was quiet for a few moments when suddenly Rover, Rock, and Grace gave a growl and headed for the door. Billy and Judy jumped up also. Billy opened the door, and out they went, followed by Hero, Spud, Alert, and Sammie. It was too late to stop the little ones. They were going to be in the heat of the chase.

Nathan called out, "I've got it, Billy. Fall, let's go see." The two followed the three, but now it was seven. Two men on horseback had stopped when they saw our lookouts. Rover, Rock, and Grace had spread out in their usual style. The four little ones joined the stance with two on each side of Rover. They made their stance also. They kept watching Grace and Rock. What Grace does now, the four will learn. Nathan and Fall approached slowly, rifles in hand. One yelled out, "We mean no harm. We just want to talk to Mister Bill."

"What for?" Nathan asked.

"We both need work and a home."

"Where are your wives?"

"Not married yet," was the reply. Biscuit rode in, slid off his pony, and took their firearms.

He then asked, "Any knives, cowboys?"

"Yes, sir." Both of the strangers handed him their hunting knives. Sunrise and Ned were waiting. They had been watching from the stables.

"Looks like all is well," Sunrise said. "Here they come. Shanghai, get behind those logs and keep an eye out for more cowboys." Most everyone was up also, wanting to see what all the fuss was about. Billy and Judy were there, too.

Jose said, "Mister Bill, I've seen these two before. They are the two men that were following the river on their way to Amarillo. They had stopped to rest and water their horses. They began to tell each other about the A.S.B. Ranch where everyone wears blue bandanas. One wanted to go to the ranch, but the other was not ready. Now it looks like they both are ready."

Judy said, "Get off your ponies, come sit and tell us your story."

"Yes, ma'am," as they lid off their horses. "My name is Fred, and this is Eddie. We are brothers from St. Louis. Our family were dirt farmers. Ma and Pa liked their farm life. We liked it, too. Me taught us to read, and one of the books we fell in love with was *The Adventure of Mister Bill*. He had a free life, no cares, just roaming the west and living off the land."

Fred said, "It was fun for a few years, but now we would like to find a home in this beautiful country. Like Mister Bill, we are good with our pistol and knives. We want to be just like him."

As they kept telling their story, Billy walked off a distance and leaned on a fence post.

Judy followed over and asked "Honey, are you all right?"

"Yes, my love, just thinking about my youth as I dreamed of the west and open spaces. No matter what the trip was, it was worth it because I found you, my love and wife." He looked over at Sunrise and Bright Eyes for they found each other, too. "Nathan," he called, "what do you think?"

"Now we have five more to add to our ranch."

"Talk to the others and decided tomorrow morning."

Early the next day, after a bite of breakfast, Uncle Ned sat them together. "If you want a place to call home and be a part of the family, raise your hand." All five raised their hands. "Your work will be hard sometimes. Here you will learn to love and laugh and spread joy. You will be dedicated to all that wear the blue bandanas. Do you understand?" All nodded. "Miss Judy will now read to you our oath to each other."

"Jose, Marie, Pedro, Fred and Eddie listen carefully. *You will be loyal to the family, everyone that wears the blue bandana. You will stand by each other through thick or thin or whatever. You will learn how to shoot both pistol and rifle.* Mama Smith, bring out the blue cloth." Each one was given a piece of fabric. "Wear the bandana at all times. Marie, you will help around the homestead. Our women do not work in the fields. If you do ride around the ranch or check the fences, do not do it alone.

Our family was growing

So was the ranch.

The Last Ride

Post:
Many years have passed, and time has taken its toll, but the love for the family will always last. The ranch was built on love and loyalty. Our Motto was:
"Love, Laugh, and Spread Joy"
Once a new person was added to the family, they never wanted to leave it. At death they were all buried on the hill overlooking the ranch.

> Together in life, together in death,
> They are riding their pony up in the sky.
> Jesus took them home.

The A.S.B Ranch would be divided into four sections, each one with an overseer. He or she would be in charge and care for their section. They would live in that section with their wife or husband and family. They would respect it like as it was their own ranch.

> Del was assigned the South Section
> Webb was assigned the North Section
> Frank was assigned the West Section
> Ben was assigned the East section.

They were given free range to manage their part of the ranch as they saw fit. Once a week, all would meet to discuss problems, make plans for the next week, or farther into what might be coming next.

Fred and Eddie were the range riders, visiting each section of the ranch once a week, reporting back to Nathan and giving a report of each section's progress or non-progress. These six men were vital to the success of the A.S.B. Ranch.

Nathan, the foreman and overseer of it all, was the real success of the ranches: ranges, horses, cattle and land protector. He thought it was all his, and in a way, it was. He took a wife named Sarah.

Uncle Ned, the runaway slave, was Billy's right-hand man. Ned was getting older, and Billy did not want him to overdo it. Their days on the trails had bonded them with brotherly respect and loyalty.

Sunrise was head of security, which was a big responsibility. It took him a long time to get over his parents' deaths. But it made him grow with more dedication and loyalty. His wife, Bright Eyes, was the apple of his eye.

Shanghai probably was the most loyal of all, for he knew if he had not been rescued from the train gang, he would have died long ago. He never forgot the train times. His attitude was—*Don't mess with anyone on this ranch that wears the blue bandana, especially Billy.*

Wolf, from the Zuni Tribe that lived in Arizona, ran out from their home land by the Spanish soldiers looking for gold, didn't know why anyone would kill another person just for gold. Or understand why anyone could rape and kill his beloved companion, Happy Face, mother of Water Fall and Bright Eyes.

Water Fall became a strong Zuni like his father, Wolf. It came time for him to find a wife, and he did. One day he and Biscuit were riding checking the fences. She came riding up, lost and frightened. He brought her home and soon married her. She was an Apache. Her name was Soso.

Biscuit, Cleo, and Shanghai worked together in keeping everyone fed. It was a chore. Mr. Wilson and Slay helped out. It was quite a team and a big job. They loved to see everyone enjoy their food.

Over the years, the A.S.B. Ranch expanded and became the largest ranch in Texas with a total of 395,000 acres. Many cowboys and cowgirls found a home on the A.S.B. They all took the oath of loyalty and wore the blue bandana. Everyone became a family member.

Rover, Billy's beloved companion and friend, lived to be eighteen-years-old. When he passed away, many tears flowed down cheeks. He was buried on the hill beside the rest of the family. He had been so loyal.

Rock and Grace lived many years after Rover passed away. When they died, we buried them beside Rover on the hill. Another sad, sad day.

Hero, Spud, Alert, and Sammie were our protectors for many, many years. All four had been trained by Rover, Rock. and Grace.

Pal, Pet, and Pal Junior all took their place in the building of A.S.B. They lived out their lifetime on the ranch as much of the family as anyone. We tied blue cloths to their saddles, and no one ever bothered them.

Judy Wilson, Mister Bill's beloved wife, gave birth to her first child on a cold winter night. She was named Judith Colean Allen. She was a beautiful girl and called Colean. She looked like her mother. As time passed, Judy gave birth to three more children, ending up with two girls and two boys. Judy was a beautiful, loving wife and dear friend to so many.

She loved to ride the range and visit with the wives and girlfriends that lived on the ranch. She could never ride alone. If Billy could not go with her, two loyal cowboys would ride along. Her trips into Pampa were a joy for her to visit the storekeepers and the good people of the town. Because of her and Billy and the reputation of the family, there was never any trouble in Pampa. A living angel she was.

Billy Allen
Billy, a young lad who fell in love with a story in a book, *The Saga of Mister Bill*, became Mister Bill. Driven by an inner desire to see the lands of the west frontier, he left his home at the age of fourteen. Inside him was a love for adventure. He could not put this aside and knew he had to go. Somehow he knew he was not traveling alone because deep inside him was someone else. He followed his heart in all endeavors. His love for the beautiful world, his fellow men and women kept him going.

In his mind, he would say, "Jesus is traveling with me." He was never afraid to travel the land. When he had a chance to help someone in need, he did as he was led. Evil had no chance when Billy was around. As he went from place to place, opportunities would arise that gave him a chance to help someone, a person or persons that were taken advantage of by evil men.

Along the way, others joined him, and he would say, "You are family now." It gave them the feeling "someone cares for me now." They began to call him Mister Bill...They all believed as long as they were one of Mister Bill's family all were safe because it was all-for-one and one-for-all.

He and his family built the largest ranch in Texas. It was a place for rest for all that came to make a home for themselves or for their family. Mister Bill gave the ranch in many ways to his family that joined him as he and Ned rode through the world of beauty for many years. After a few years, Jesus led him back to his childhood home.

His love for family started when he was just a lad, a youngster that was fed love by his mother and father. David Allen, his father, was an Irish gentleman that came across the Atlantic Ocean in hopes of finding an opportunity for a free life in a free world. As he stepped off the boat, his eyes fell on a beauty by the name of Ruth Smith, a southern lady of grace. They fell in love. She left her family to be with David, wherever he wanted to roam.

Ruth Smith and David Allen were the cornerstone that held Billy up all through his life until the day he fell off his horse.

His eyes looked up to Heaven as an angel took his hand and said, "It is time to go home now." It was – HIS LAST RIDE.